A percentage of the profits from *The Brother's Creed* series will be donated to Colors of Heroes®.

**Freedom is never free!**

Colors of Heroes is a 501c3 nonprofit foundation dedicated to rebuilding confidence for combat wounded veterans and gold star families through new relationships and outdoor adventures.

Learn more at: *www.colorsofheroes.org*

# BATTLEBORN

## THE BROTHER'S CREED
### BOOK 2

*Lending*
*you too are*
*battle born!*

Josh C. Ch

## JOSHUA C. CHADD

Contact the author via email at:
*joshuacchadd@outlook.com*

ISBN-13: 978-1548405960

ISBN-10: 1548405965

*Aunty Brenda,*
*I know you can get through this with God and your family by your side. You too are battle born!*
*#Brendastrong*

*~~~*

*We've been through a lot over the years and you've always stood by me when times were tough. You were there for me when it felt like the whole world was against me. It's been a privilege to stand by you as we've both grown into men over the years. Through thick or thin we've kept and strengthened our bond. I couldn't imagine life without my 'little' brother!*
*You'll always be my closest friend and the best brother a guy could ask for.*
*This one's for you, Caleb!*

# PROLOGUE

The summer sun sank below the Bighorn Mountains as a string of vehicles drove north on I-90. The caravan was led by a massive big rig with a makeshift plow attached to the front. It was the perfect behemoth for pushing vehicles aside and also did quite a number on the undead. There were six vehicles in the caravan, consisting of four trucks, a minivan, and the big rig with twenty survivors ranging from middle-aged men and women to children. The fourth vehicle in line was a maroon Chevy Avalanche with a twenty-year-old man behind the wheel.

Tank hung up his cell phone and set it on the dash, turning the music back on. *Generation Dead* by Five Finger Death Punch resumed playing. Adjusting the rearview mirror, he looked at his reflection. Keen gray eyes stared back at him. His short brown hair was in need of a good wash and his beard was quickly growing wild. He regretted not shaving the weekend before the apocalypse.

He'd always been a little bigger than other men—not only in stature, but with a few extra pounds as well. However, the apocalypse was turning out to be the best weight loss program— only five days in and he'd already lost a few pounds. Another week of this and he'd be approaching a weight appropriate for his frame.

*That is if I can survive another week,* he thought.

He looked out the windshield at the end-of-the-world scene before him and smiled. Abandoned vehicles were scattered on the interstate, undead slowly wandering between them. Unlike other people, the apocalypse didn't mean the end of the world for him but rather the start of a new life. He wouldn't miss his dead-end job bartending at the Blue Crab or his so-called friends in Fort Collins, Colorado. This could be a grand adventure, the beginning of something truly great. And when the Andderson brothers joined him, the Wolf Pack would be back together and nothing would stand in their way!

One thing kept this situation from being the best damn turn of events for him in a while. His mom was gone, and although she'd passed away over a year ago, it still weighed on him. Lynda Hook had been an amazing woman, far more so than most recognized. She was the one who'd always supported him in all he did and was always there for him. He missed her, although it was probably better that she didn't have to live through this shit-storm. His dad, Grant, was still alive last he knew, opting to stay in a small town in the San Juan Mountains. Grant was a good man and more prepared than most, with a wide collection of guns and in a great location for survival. Tank had almost gone south to weather the apocalypse with his dad; however, he'd escaped north of Fort Collins and he wasn't about to go back.

Losing his mom and being away from his dad wasn't enough to make the smile disappear from his face entirely, even though it did dampen his spirits. He readjusted the mirror and subtly glanced at the two smokin' hot women in the backseat. Chloe was a brunette with soft features, full lips, and a pout permanently glued to her face. He didn't like her at all. From what he'd seen, the pout was not only a facial feature but personified her whiney personality. Eva however, was the opposite. While she looked and dressed somewhat gothic, she was one of the most genuinely cheerful women he'd ever met. She had medium-length black hair—the tips dyed purple—and the body of someone who worked out often.

*I hope she survives long enough for me to get to know her,* he thought.

The man sitting next to him in the passenger seat was someone he knew would get along well with the brothers. Garett had some serious five o'clock shadow and long blonde hair which he had pulled into a ponytail. He was a quiet man and a hunter, with his own collection of guns.

Big Bertha—as they called the semi-trailer truck leading the caravan—made a grinding sound and a few seconds later the big rig rolled to a stop. Smoke billowed from the engine. The rest of the caravan stopped and four people piled out of the semi. Three took up a defensive position, shooting at the undead closing in, while the fourth went around to the front of Big Bertha.

"Morons," Tank said under his breath.

*Don't they listen to anything? The damn things are attracted to sound,* he thought.

"What is it?" Chloe asked, worry in her voice.

"Just three idiots making enough noise to draw every undead within a mile," Tank said.

"Are you always such an ass?" Chloe asked.

"Does the sun rise in the east?" Tank said.

"Figures," Chloe said, "The end of the world and I get stuck with him."

"Just be quiet, Chloe," Eva said, then turned to Tank. "Can you see anything?"

"Not really. The engine is smoking, but could be nothing," Tank said.

"Or could be bad," Garett said, grabbing the AR-15 at his side and sticking it out the open window.

Garett began taking out the undead that were closing in on the caravan, most of his suppressed shots finding their mark. Tank looked down at the Colt 1911 handgun holstered on his right hip. It had been a high school graduation present from his dad. The handgun was black with rosewood grips and the skeleton of a dragon painted on the slide. He felt better with the handgun on his side and three extra magazines shoved into the various pockets of his green cargo pants.

It was cooling down outside, the sun having disappeared below the mountains. He slipped his black jacket on overtop his Five Finger Death Punch t-shirt and looked out the window. The undead were mainly taken care of, for the time being, but if they didn't get that big rig rolling soon, they'd be in trouble.

"I'm gonna go see what's wrong," Garett said after finding nothing else to shoot.

"I'll stay here and be ready to pick you up if all hell breaks loose," Tank said.

"Thanks," Garett said, getting out of the truck.

Looking forward, Tank wondered what had happened to stop them dead in their tracks. Until now, he'd thought Big Bertha was indestructible, especially after Casper. But what did he expect? The world was ending, and at this point if things *weren't* going to hell that would be more of a concern.

"Tell us about your friends you were talking to on the phone earlier," Eva said.

"They've been my best friends since middle school," Tank said, "two of the only *real* friends I've ever had. They're brothers and way kickass. It'll be good to meet up with them since they'll be rollin' heavy."

"Rollin' heavy?" Eva asked.

"Yeah, like loaded," he said, glancing back at her, but he could tell she still didn't know what he was talking about. "They'll have a lot of guns."

"Oh," Eva said, "that'll be nice."

*You have no idea,* he thought as he noticed Garett walking back toward them. *Hopefully, whatever's wrong won't be too serious.*

A shot sounded in the darkness. Garett fell against the side of the green Ford Ranger in front of them and slid to the ground, blood soaking his shirt.

"Get down!" Tank yelled to the girls as the night lit up with the sounds of gunfire. The windshield shattered as bullets peppered the side of his truck. Flashes of light from the muzzles of the guns shone in the encroaching darkness on a hilltop to the east.

"Hold on!" Tank roared as he slammed the truck into gear.

The tires squealed on the pavement as he pushed the pedal to the floor and the truck jerked forward. Bullets continued to slam into his truck and he heard glass shatter in the backseat. One of the girls screamed.

*We need to get the hell out of here!* he thought, swerving off the interstate and into a ditch on the left. The truck easily drove down the small embankment and onto more level ground, but out of nowhere, the green Ranger sped off the interstate right in front of him. He tried to slam on the brakes, but it was no use. He plowed into the side of the smaller truck and the airbags deployed, slamming into his face as the truck came to a screeching halt.

Dazed, he opened the door and stumbled out, going down to his knees. His nose was bleeding and he had small cuts in at least a dozen places. Looking back, he groaned. The entire front end of his truck was pulverized and he wouldn't be driving it anywhere. A bullet whizzed by overhead and he burst into action. Rising to his feet, he opened the back door and Chloe stumbled out, bleeding from a cut on her forehead. Tank reached in and tried to pull Eva from the backseat, but she was still buckled in. Climbing inside, he reached for the seat belt but stopped short. Half of her neck had been blown off.

Cursing, he quickly climbed back out. Two survivors, Bob and Selena, got out of the Ranger and began to stumble toward the edge of a hill to the west. Tank hauled Chloe to her feet and they followed. Bullets started to punch the dirt all around them and they ran faster. A bullet slammed into Bob's back and he fell to the ground. Selena slowed to help him.

"Don't stop!" Tank yelled. "Keep moving!"

The three of them made it to the lip of the hill and ran over the edge, starting down the gradual decline. They continued to run over the barren, hilly terrain as darkness continued to grow. Descending another hillside, Tank stumbled to a stop after ten minutes of running. He couldn't run any further without having an asthma attack and his inhaler was back in the truck. The girls weren't faring any better. Both were bent over, taking heaving breaths.

"What do we do now?" Chloe asked when she'd mostly caught her breath.

"I honestly have no idea," Tank said, "But we can't stay out here in the open. We need to find some cover and—damn."

"What?" Selena asked.

"The brothers," Tank said. He reached into his pants pocket, searching for his phone. It wasn't there. Checking his jacket, he came up empty.

"Oh, come on," he said.

"What now?" Chloe asked. She looked like she was about to have a breakdown.

"My phone's in the damn truck," Tank said. "Either of you have one?"

"No," Chloe said.

"I have mine," Selena said, pulling out her phone.

Tank grabbed the phone and hesitated. What the hell was James's number again? He racked his brain and finally came up with it. Punching the number into the phone, he hit the call button just as the screen blacked out. He held down the power button and the dead battery screen popped up.

"No chance you have a portable charger?"

The girls shook their heads.

"I figured as much. The brothers shouldn't—"

"Are those headlights?" Selena asked, looking back the way they'd come.

Tank looked back and cursed. "No, those are flashlights," he said. "They're hunting us!"

The three of them stumbled into the darkness toward the Bighorn Mountains in the distance.

# 1
# BURNS

Headlights illuminated three zombies next to the gas pumps and James slowed his white Dodge RAM truck. Connor hopped out while it was still rolling forward, AR-15 at his left shoulder. With three shots, he had them on the ground. Using the flashlight mounted on his AR, he scanned for more as he signaled his brother to pull forward. James parked his truck and jumped out, 1911 handgun at the ready, meeting his brother at the back of the vehicle.

James wore his customary Kryptek camouflage and had his short brown hair hidden under a ball cap. His hazel eyes scanned the darkness through his glasses, looking for any threats. Standing next to his brother made James look smaller than he actually was. Connor stood at six foot, four inches taller, and had at least another ten pounds of muscle on him.

"Looks clear. Bring 'em in," Connor said.

He wore an outfit similar to his brother's, but his shaved head was bare of a hat and sported night vision goggles instead. While James wore a long-sleeved Kryptek shirt against the night's chill, Connor wore a t-shirt, his muscled arms with the word "persevere" tattooed on his left forearm showing in the light from the truck.

Taking the radio out of a pocket on his tactical vest, James pressed the button. "Target is clear," he spoke into the receiver.

"Roger that, boys," Ana said teasingly over the radio.

He was still surprised at her slight Russian accent even though she'd lived her whole life in America. He hadn't learned much about her since this morning when Ana, Alexis and Emmett had convinced them to tag along. Emmett was Alexis's dad—that was plain by the resemblance—and they'd picked Ana up a few days before. The events surrounding that were still foggy for James since they hadn't shared much, but he'd gathered that Alexis had lost her mother around that time too.

Alexis... now she was something. She was skilled with a gun and seemed completely unfazed at almost being fed to zombies the night before. He knew she had to be struggling with it in her own way, but outwardly she was holding it together surprisingly well. Emmett had done a good job of raising her right. That didn't come as a surprise since he was a Marine and a man after James's own heart. In fact, Emmett reminded James of his father in quite a few ways.

Memories flooded his mind—hunting with his dad in the mountains of Colorado; learning how to build camp, start a fire, and properly care for the meat and hide; learning to respect the animals and the land they hunted; and learning to be a man of his word and to treat everyone with respect, even when he didn't like or agree with them.

He was pulled from his thoughts as a set of headlights exited the interstate and a black Ford F-450 pulled up to the pumps opposite them. James wiped a single tear from his eye and put on a smile.

Emmett Wolfe stepped out of the driver's seat, his dark brown duster settling around him. Grabbing his cowboy hat off the dash, he set it on his head, covering short-cropped black hair. He gazed into the darkness, his hawk-like features accentuated by the low light and the pale line of a scar that stood out on his left cheek. Walking around the front of the truck, he held his Beretta handgun at his chest.

"We good here?" Emmett asked, continuing to survey the darkness.

"Yes, sir," Connor said, taking up a position at the back of the Ford where he could cover the girls while they got out.

"It's clear girls," Emmett said.

Alexis stepped out and around the front of the truck, smiling at James. She was beautiful, with brunette hair pulled into a messy bun on top of her head, blue eyes looking like gems in the darkness, and a SCAR assault rifle at her shoulder. Despite himself, his heart gave a small flutter.

*Are you serious right now? You've only known her for a day and already you like her?* he asked his heart. *Damn thing must be broken.* That thought sparked painful memories of the past few days and he realized the last statement was too close for comfort.

Ana climbed out of the backseat, her auburn hair pulled into a ponytail and her green eyes reflecting the light. She walked over to stand watch next to Connor, holding her Springfield XDM handgun close.

They began to fuel up their trucks. James walked around to the bed of his truck and opened the tailgate, sitting down. Pulling up his left pant leg and unwrapping the gauze, he checked his gunshot wound. It hadn't bothered him since his brother cleaned and wrapped it yesterday morning.

"Can I take a look?" Alexis asked, walking over.

"Sure," James said.

She set her rifle on the tailgate and pulled out a flashlight from a pouch on her belt. She bent down, prodding the two small holes with experienced fingers. It hurt him slightly but wasn't terrible. Clicking the flashlight off, she straightened up, replacing it at her belt.

"Doesn't look like much damage was done, although there's a fair amount of bruising. What'd you do?" Alexis asked, picking up her rifle.

"Someone tried to kill me, only they failed quite spectacularly. They did manage to catch my leg with a part of the shotgun blast though," James said, putting his pant leg back down and standing up to close the tailgate. "Thanks for looking at it. You seem to know what you're doing."

"Thanks. I spent the last two years training to be a paramedic and recently took my licensing exam."

"Did you pass?"

"I did. I was actually going to start work Monday. Then all this happened."

"Yeah, the outbreak really messed life up, didn't it?"

"You got that right."

"Well, it's good to have someone along who knows what they're doing when one of us gets hurt," James said, going over to top off the tank of his truck.

"Thanks," Alexis said, smiling, and walked over to her dad's truck.

"Hear anything from your friend?" Emmett asked as he hung up the nozzle.

"Yeah, a couple hours ago," James said, "He's south of Sheridan and planning to stop at the Montana border. If we travel through the night, we should catch up with them by morning."

"Good," Emmett said. "More people might not be a bad thing."

"Or it might be a horrible thing," Connor said from the back of the truck.

"He has a point," Ana said.

"We'll see," James said. "We need to get to Tank first. Then we can figure out the rest."

"Is that his real name?" Alexis asked.

"No," James said, thinking back to years prior. "It's his nickname. All three of us have one."

"Were you guys in a gang or something?" Ana asked.

"Something like that," James said, chuckling.

"So what are they?" Alexis asked.

"Mine's Hunter, because, well, I like to hunt and it sounds cool," James said, just then realizing how dorky it sounded. "I swear that sounded better in my head."

The girls laughed.

"And yours?" Ana asked Connor.

"Iceman," he said simply.

"And?" Ana asked when it was clear he wasn't going to elaborate.

"Because my heart is frozen and I don't give a shit," Connor said.

"So like a honey badger crossed with Elsa," Ana said.

James burst out laughing and the rest joined in.

"Not quite," Connor said, smiling slightly. "I got it in the Marines and it stuck. Made sense when I started flying, too."

"Why did it make sense then?" Alexis asked.

"Are you kidding me?" James asked. "You've never seen *Top Gun*?"

"No," Alexis said.

"Really? And you call yourself an American?" James asked.

"To be fair," Emmett said, "she did watch it when she was younger. I made sure—"

Groaning could be heard from the direction of the gas station building and they all moved into action at once, raising their guns.

"You girls good for now on a bathroom?" Emmett asked.

"I can make it another hour," Alexis said, getting into the truck.

"Me too," Ana said, climbing in.

"Let's go then," James said.

Loading into their respective trucks, they drove out of the station and back onto I-80. Connor turned the radio on. The iPod that was hooked up to the truck automatically started playing their Apocalypse Road Trip playlist and *Zombie* by We As Human blared through the speakers. With music playing and headlights cutting through the darkness, they continued on their way, one step closer to their destination.

James still couldn't believe the events of the day before. From both of their parents and Felicia being killed to rescuing Emmett and the girls to Tank still being alive, it had gone from 'nothing to live for' to 'maybe there's still hope' rather quickly. It'd been a rush, going from that low of a low to the high of saving three people and finding out that their best friend was alive. But now the high was wearing off and reality was settling in. Their parents were dead, forever gone from this world, and there was nothing he could do to get them back.

*But they're not gone,* said a small voice in his head.

He ignored that voice, which was becoming increasingly easier with each passing hour. Why should he hope? There might be something to live for today, but what about when more people died tomorrow? What about when Ana died? Or Emmett? Alexis? Connor? Even just *thinking* about losing his brother made him want to cry.

*No, I can't think like that... but what if? What if he did die? Then I will end it all, taking out as many as I can.*

As the night continued, his thoughts strayed down darker paths, leaving him feeling like he wanted to cry—but he couldn't. If he opened the floodgates now, he might never get them closed. So he buried the feelings, trying his best to put on a happy face. It didn't work, but at least he held back the tears. Glancing over at his brother, he could tell Connor was struggling also.

*I need to stay strong for him,* he thought. *Even though he may handle this better, he's still my little brother.*

"You okay, bro?" James asked, watching as the headlights shone on a plethora of abandoned vehicles with a few zombies roaming around.

"What do you think?" Connor asked, a bitter edge to his voice.

"I think we're both in a bad place right now..." He wanted to say more to somehow help them both work through this, but the conversation withered inside him.

Settling into his seat, he let his mind wander while he drove through the obstacle course that was the interstate. Once they met up with Tank, they would continue making their way to Alaska. It would take some work, but after they were all safely at their remote lodge they could have a somewhat normal life. His thoughts drifted off as the night deepened.

He was thinking about how good a Canadian bacon and pineapple pizza sounded when he stiffened in his seat, headlights shining on hundreds of eyes—eyes belonging to a horde of zombies. He cursed loudly.

Connor jerked awake, reaching for a weapon as the truck rolled to a stop and the zombies began shambling toward the light. Connor registered the scene in a matter of seconds and grabbed the radio off the dash.

"Emmett, you copy?" Connor said.

"Roger that," Emmett said. "What you got up there?"

"A whole lotta zombies."

"Can we get through 'em?"

"No way. We need to get outta here, fast."

James had the truck in reverse and was backing up, but with all the vehicles on the road it was slow going in the dark. The zombies were only five yards away and closing, rather quickly by zombie standards. Finally, James found an opening and whipped the truck into it, turning around.

"Where's the nearest exit?" James asked his brother.

Connor pulled out a road atlas and began to study it. "Where are we?"

"Just crossed into Wyoming on I-80."

"Have we gone past Burns?"

"Yes, a couple miles back."

"Good, we—"

"Connor, you there?" Ana asked over the radio.

"Roger," Connor replied.

"We found an exit, number 386. It'll take us north on highway 213."

"That's what I found too. Go through Burns and get on I-25 at Chugwater."

"Yep," Ana said. "Guess we'll lead. Plan to stop in Burns for a bathroom break."

"Roger that," Connor said, sticking the atlas between the seats.

They rode in silence for the next couple of minutes until they saw the exit and the black Ford waiting for them. The truck exited the interstate and James followed.

"It seems like there are more of them now," James said.

"Of course there are. Fewer survivors usually means more zombies," Connor responded.

"It just seems like it happened all of a sudden. Maybe the last few towns holding out have all turned."

"Wouldn't surprise me. Things are going to hell real quick."

James nodded. How true that statement really was. Was this hell on earth? Was this the End Times? Or was any of that even true? His beliefs still *felt* true, but doubt was gnawing at him. That worried him more than the zombies ever could.

After two miles, they arrived at the tiny town of Burns with a population of three hundred and one, according to the sign. The highway continued north, passing the town on the eastern side. In the darkness, it was hard to tell how big the town actually was. What stuck out to James most was the faint light coming from a large building just to the left of the highway. Emmett came to a stop in front of him. James pulled alongside and Connor rolled down his window.

"What do you think?" James asked Emmett.

"Not sure what to think," Emmett replied, studying the partially fenced-in field and playground on the east side of the large building.

"Looks like a school," James said, noticing the buses parked out front.

"Maybe they'll have medical supplies and food in the cafeteria," Alexis said.

"Those lights mean someone is in there or recently has been," Connor said.

"True," James said. "The horde was south of here on the interstate, heading east. We should be good for a few minutes, but I don't think we should stick around long. The question is, do we move on or check out the lights?"

"All I know is if I don't use the bathroom soon," Ana said, "I'll need a new pair of pants."

"Can't you just squat behind the truck?" Connor asked.

Ana gave him a particular look. "I *could*, but I'd much rather not."

"I say some of us go in and check it out while the rest stay with the vehicles, just in case," James said. "We can take the radios. Then, if the horde approaches, we can get out quickly."

Emmett nodded. "Sounds good."

They pulled forward, turning onto Fourth Street, and stopped in the small parking lot on the north side of the road. There were only three cars there and no zombies in sight. Another large parking lot sat farther to the west, with two buses parked by the main entrance to the school. Turning the truck off, James grabbed a set of night vision goggles from the backseat. He stepped out of the truck, turning his Kryptek ball cap backwards. After putting the NVGs onto his head, he grabbed his AR. He was glad he'd already adjusted the NVG optics so they didn't interfere with his glasses. His brother walked around the front of the truck and they stood there, looking toward the school.

They were dressed in their full Kryptek camouflage outfits, decked out with their tactical vests, side arms, tomahawks, NVGs and suppressed AR-15s. They'd attached infrared lasers to their AR rails, opposite the flashlights, since they wouldn't be able to aim through their scopes with the NVGs. The IR lasers were part of the loot they'd gathered from the courthouse basement in Nebraska.

Emmett turned his truck off and the night was plunged into darkness. James flipped the optics down over his eyes and his view was bathed in a green light, the darkness becoming illuminated. Every time he put those on it was almost like he was traveling to an alien planet with a green sun. Turning his infrared laser on, a faint green line pointed from the end of his barrel. He brought the AR to his shoulder and tried to get used to aiming with the laser. It took him a second but he quickly got the hang of it.

Sweeping the surrounding area, laser pointing where he was aiming, he came up empty. It seemed like there were no zombies around, which was odd and put him on edge.

"I don't see anything," James said softly.

"Me neither," Connor responded. "We need to keep our heads on a swivel."

"I agree."

Emmett walked over. "You two go in. The girls and I'll wait out here and keep an eye on things."

"Roger that," Connor said.

"Just what I was thinking," James said.

Emmett walked back to his truck, grabbed his suppressed 6.5 Creedmoor custom rifle from the backseat, and climbed onto the topper. Sitting down at the shooting bench, he attached a small night vision device on the end of his scope. Alexis stayed next to Emmett's truck while Ana went over to James's truck, both of them wearing NVGs.

"Good luck," Alexis said as the brothers moved off.

"Thanks," James said and led the way to the school's side entrance, stopping outside the door. "You ready?"

"Always."

James opened the door and Connor swept into the school. Entering behind his brother, James examined the hallway with a quick glance and then began looking for threats. Since he was right-handed, he focused more heavily on the left side, and he knew Connor would be focusing more on the right since he was left-handed. They took a few steps into the hallway, then stopped side-by-side and examined it more closely. This wing of the building was a long hallway with lockers lining both sides and doors every twenty feet. The hallway was neat, not how it would be if zombies had rampaged through the place. At the end of the hall there was a set of glass double doors, and through those doors the faint light shone.

"Let's check 'em all," James said. Connor nodded. There was no sense in running through the building and then finding out they had enemies at their backs.

James went to the door on the left side of the hall and posted up next to it. Connor came up and James opened the door for him as Connor swept into the room. James followed behind. Inside was a classroom with no threats. It was eerie. Nothing was wrong. Even though the apocalypse had only been in full swing for a few days, they were used to seeing places trashed, with items scattered around in a state of disrepair and usually a body or two, or at least a good amount of blood. Yet this classroom looked like the rest of the hallway they'd seen—untouched.

They left the room and repeated the process on the door across the hall. It was the same. By the look of the classrooms, James concluded this was an elementary school. As they exited the room, he shuddered at the thought of all these kids having to live through this horror. In all their travels so far they'd yet to come across any children as zombies and he was glad for it. He couldn't imagine having kids of his own right now. How on earth would he protect them? What would it be like for someone to lose their child to something like this? The world really was going to hell.

Moving down the hall, they continued to check each room. The only thing they found of use was in a small room at the end of the hall on the left—the nurses' station. Grabbing a backpack from one of the lockers, James emptied the contents onto the floor and went back into the nurses' station. He gathered up all the medical supplies and the two first aid kits and shoved them into the backpack, which he threw over his shoulder.

Through the glass double doors was a large, square room that must be the cafeteria, judging by the tables. There was an entrance across the cafeteria that looked identical to the one they were standing in, and to the left was a set of wooden double doors. Underneath those double doors, light pooled out like liquid gold. All of the tables had been moved in front of the doors, making it impossible to get through them without climbing over the barricade. If James had to guess, it looked like a decent attempt to slow or stop zombies from getting in. More than likely, there would be survivors in that room. But how many? And what kind—ones needing help or a bullet to the head?

Cautiously, they entered the cafeteria, heads on a swivel. Finally, he saw what they'd come to expect. There were items scattered around the floor—food wrappers, lunch boxes, backpacks and school books. In the middle of the room, they stopped and looked around again. To their right sat a pair of doors leading outside to a playground and soccer field next to the school. To their left were the doors with light underneath and a small room next to it. That room would be the kitchen.

It turned out that the kitchen had been ransacked and looted, with not a single edible item left. It even lacked the refrigerators, ovens and microwaves.

*They moved it all,* James thought as they backed out of the room. The brothers stood by the tables, the sound of soft voices drifting to them through the wooden doors.

"Survivors," James whispered.

"What's the play?" Connor asked.

James was about to respond when he heard a sound behind them. Turning around and crouching down, he aimed his AR at the doors leading outside. Through the small windows, they could see a group of a dozen armed men coming through the outside set of doors. They were a mismatched band of survivors, carrying anything from a sharpened broom handle to an M16 rifle, and all had flashlights. The brothers moved as one, jumping over the counter and into the kitchen. The group's hushed conversation drifted to them as the second set of doors opened and they entered the cafeteria.

"Why are we this paranoid?" asked one of the men, hauling a large black garbage bag over his shoulder. "We haven't even seen anything like what the news talked about."

"It could be some sort of elaborate prank," another man said. He was armed with an old bolt-action rifle.

"Till the news comes back on and we can find out more, we'll continue to prepare for the worst," said the lead man, who was carrying a baseball bat.

"I ain't never trusted the government and I ain't bout to start now," said the redneck armed with the M16.

"That's your own issue, Randy," said the man with the baseball bat. "They said to stay indoors until help comes, so that's what we'll do. Even going over to the high school like we did could be dangerous. We don't even know what's going on."

"Yes, but we needed the food," another of the men said.

The man with the baseball bat climbed over the tables in front of the doors and knocked three times before pausing to knock again. The doors opened and James peeked up for a brief look. The room was packed full of men, women, and a lot of children. There were tents set up inside the large gym, along with all the cooking appliances from the kitchen. They handed the bags to the people inside the room and then followed, closing the doors after them.

"We need to move. Now," Connor whispered. "These people are sitting ducks, and when one of them turns it'll be a bloody massacre."

"We need to warn them about the horde coming this way," James said.

"They're not our problem!"

"We can't just leave 'em!"

The door cracked open and James cursed under his breath.

"Is someone out there?" asked the man with the baseball bat as he peered into the dark cafeteria.

James crouched, perfectly still, not daring to move a muscle as the beam from the man's flashlight swept the room. The man grunted and shook his head, closing the door again. James sighed and looked at his brother, who returned his stare angrily.

"Whatever," James said, standing. "Let's go."

Jumping over the counter, James kept his eyes on the door to make sure no one else came out, which was why he didn't see the woman coming from the opposite hallway until her flashlight beam fell on him. James aimed at her as she screamed. Connor took three steps toward her when the doors burst opened.

James swung back around to face the eight armed men standing in the doorway and quickly found the highest priority target—the man with the

M16. Connor made it to the woman and grabbed her before she could react. Letting his AR drop to his side on the sling, he drew his 1911 handgun and pressed the barrel to the side of her head.

"Let's not do anything rash now," James said, eyeing the men standing in front of him. Their expressions ranged from fear to shock to barely contained rage. He focused on the angry men more than the rest.

"We ain't the ones with hostages," said Randy, the redneck with the M16.

"Who are you?" asked the man with the baseball bat.

"Just two men passing through," James said.

"Why'd you come here?" Baseball Bat asked.

"To investigate the light."

"I told you we shouldn't use them lights," Randy said.

"Shut up, Randy," said another man.

"We don't want any trouble," James said.

"Then let her go," Baseball Bat said.

"No," Connor growled.

*Great,* James thought. *If he keeps this up, we'll end up having to shoot our way out.*

"We came to investigate the light," James said again, "and to warn anyone here. There's a horde of over a hundred zombies coming this way from Cheyenne."

"So now yer tryin' to save us?" Randy asked.

"Why the hell should we trust you?" asked another man.

James ignored them and locked eyes with Baseball Bat, since he seemed the most reasonable. He was a middle-aged man with receding brown hair and bushy eyebrows that framed intelligent brown eyes. He carried himself with authority and James knew this was the man he had to convince.

"Lay down your weapons and we'll lay ours down," Baseball Bat said.

"But Peter—" one of the men began.

"We do *not* want to start a bloodbath," Peter said. "Lay 'em down and we'll do likewise."

James glanced over at his brother and knew he wouldn't lay down his weapon. He didn't trust them and James didn't either—in fact, they didn't trust anyone right now. He opened his mouth to respond but stopped short, hearing a barely audible voice come over the radio that was tucked into his tactical vest.

"James, the horde is on the west side of town," Ana said. "We can hear screaming and Emmett says he sees dozens of them between the houses. You need to get out of there. The zombies are coming."

# 2
## FIELD TRIP

"We don't have time for this pissin' contest!" James said, lowering his AR and flipping the NVGs up. "Connor, let her go."

His brother looked at him and hesitated.

*Just do it, bro!*

"Fine," Connor said, releasing her and holstering his handgun. Immediately, she ran past James and began to climb over the tables toward the men.

"Now, we *all* need to get out of here," James said. "Quietly gather everyone and get them to the buses parked outside." Randy opened his mouth to respond, but James shot him a look. "Do you want to die trapped in here?"

"He might be right," Peter said reluctantly. "They have no reason to lie. Gather everyone and let's get them to the buses."

"What do we tell the kids?" asked a woman with short blonde hair, walking up from behind the men.

"Tell them we're going on a field trip," Peter said.

"Stay quiet," James said, "but you'll want to move fast. Don't start up any of the buses till everyone is out."

Connor jogged past him toward the hallway they'd come from. James ran to catch up with him.

"You're gonna want to stay and help them, aren't you?" Connor spat.

"We don't have a choice," James said.

"We always have a choice. And your choices are going to get us killed! Do you want our parents' deaths to be in vain?"

"Their deaths would be in vain if we *didn't* do something more than just stay alive!"

"That's all there is to do now. Stay alive!" Connor yelled, slamming through the doors and exiting the school as he ran to the trucks.

James hesitated at the exit. *Is he right? Am I going to get us killed?* No, he knew this was the right thing to do. If they just worried about survival, what kind of life would that be? Would it even be a life worth living? He knew in his heart that this was what needed to be done. There was no choice; he'd been called to help those in need. The thought was like cold water being poured over a sunburn. He still had his faith, and no matter how angry or hurt he was, he still believed. There *was* more to life than just surviving. Jogging through the doors, he felt some of the pain in his heart fade—not much, but it was a start.

Outside, Connor was already at their truck, climbing onto the topper. While James didn't have an awesome shooting bench welded to the top of his topper, it still offered a superior view compared to the ground. James ran over to Alexis at the side of

Emmett's truck, tossing the backpack through the open window into the backseat.

"Here are some medical supplies," he said. "How bad is it out here?"

"Pretty bad," Alexis responded. "There are at least a hundred of them and they're heading this way." Screams and sporadic gunfire sounded from the town in the distance, accentuating her point. "What happened in there?"

"There are survivors—a lot of 'em—and they have kids. They're gonna load into buses and we're gonna lead 'em outta here."

"Can we trust them?" Alexis asked.

"Yeah, at least I think so," James said.

"So what you're saying is we need to keep an eye on them?" Ana asked from next to his truck.

"Yes, and the school is clear if you want to use the restroom," James said.

"I already took care of that," Ana said.

"I thought—"

"Over there!" Connor said from the topper. He pointed at the larger parking lot to the west where the two buses sat. People had begun streaming out of the school from the main entrance, heading toward the buses. Peter stood halfway between the vehicles and the school, ushering them forward.

"So far, so good," James said. The first bus was full and the second was getting loaded when the first bus's engine roared to life, shattering the relative quiet of the night. "Ah, hell."

"Here they come!" Emmett said, sighting in on the zombies beginning to shamble over their way.

"Alexis, keep them from getting too close," James said as he moved into action.

"Where are you going?" she asked.

"To help."

Without looking back at his brother, he took off across the small plot of cultured grass between their parking lot and the larger one. In the distance, a huge group of zombies began heading toward the school bus with its engine running and lights on. There was another school the zombies would have to pass before getting to them. They should be able to hold them off until the rest of the survivors loaded into the buses. Behind him, a suppressed gunshot went off in the night, followed a second later by another. Connor and Emmett had gone to work.

James ran up to Peter. "What the hell?"

"I told Greg not to start it yet," Peter said.

"We need to hurry these people up," James said. "The zombies are coming."

Peter began shouting orders to hurry the kids up. A few of them didn't want to leave the school and go outside. James couldn't blame them, but they didn't have time for this. He ran over to the entrance, getting the attention of the blonde-haired woman from before.

"You need to get them to the buses *now*," James told her. "I don't care if you have to drag 'em!"

"But they—" she began.

"I just told you I don't care. You need to get them to the buses or they'll be torn apart and eaten alive." James said the last part rather loudly, hoping the kids would hear.

*That should motivate them to move,* he thought smugly.

But it had the opposite effect as kids began to scream and cry. A little dark-haired girl around seven years old ran inside and the woman Connor had held hostage ran in after her.

"Well, that did *not* help at all," Blondie informed him.

"I can see that," he said. "Time to try plan B."

Jogging over to a little boy, he picked him up, ignoring his kicks and screams. He ran over to the closest bus, handing him off to one of the men inside. Going back, he picked up a younger girl and repeated the process. She went more willingly, although she was crying now.

*Maybe I shouldn't have mentioned them getting eaten.*

Returning to Blondie, he was happy to see that most of the kids were reluctantly following her in a line toward the bus. He guessed that after seeing some of their friends being hauled off by the big scary man, they'd decided walking would be easier—that or Blondie had told them something to get them moving. He liked to think it was the former.

"I thought you told them they're going on a field trip." James said to Blondie as they walked the kids to the bus.

"We did, but they aren't stupid," she responded, "just young."

"Well, good work so far."

"Why are you helping us?" she asked, looking at him curiously when they arrived at the bus.

"I was taught to help people," James responded. "I lost myself with everything that's been going on. But seeing all these kids in there... they don't deserve this."

He glanced at Peter who was coming toward them, a worried look on his face.

"We don't have enough room," he said, looking at the group of twenty-some standing next to the bus.

"Are there any more buses?" James asked, looking around.

There were only three vehicles in the parking lot over by their trucks that would hold a maximum of fifteen people. They could possibly shove some of them in the beds of their trucks, but that many? There wouldn't be enough room.

"Yes," Peter said, "over at the high school."

James looked toward the high school and the zombies beginning to swarm the lawn. They were running out of time.

"Where at?" James asked.

"Around the back of the building," Peter said.

"Let's go then!" James said.

Peter hesitated only a second, then took off across the parking lot, heading toward the high school. James followed. Most of the zombies were sticking to the road and the front of the school, so the back of the building should be mostly clear. He came around the corner of the building just behind Peter. There were a dozen zombies lumbering in their direction between them and the school buses. His AR was to his shoulder in a flash and he aimed at the closest one, laser resting on its head. He put a bullet in its brain. As the first one was falling to the ground, he was already swinging onto the next one. Thirteen more shots and all the zombies lay on the ground, blood slowly oozing from their heads.

"Let's go," James said. The way to the buses was now clear. "Are the keys in 'em?"

"Not these," Peter said. "They should be in the shed." At the shed, Peter entered a code into the padlock while James kept watch.

*You shouldn't be here! You should be with your brother!* said a voice in his head.

He knew the voice was right, at least partially. Helping these people was right as well, but he *had* run off rather recklessly. He and his brother were a team and that didn't work when one just up and abandoned the other. He'd have to apologize to Connor when he got back.

Peter cursed.

"What now?" James asked, glancing back at him.

"I forgot the combination," Peter said.

"Stand back." James said and aimed at the padlock but missed, blowing a hole in the door. He cursed, shot again, and this time blew the padlock apart.

Peter opened the door and grabbed a keychain off the wall. "Got 'em."

They ran to the nearest bus and Peter climbed into the driver's seat while James sat in the front row. The bus roared to life and Peter drove over the lawn in a wide U-turn, heading toward the other buses. James cursed when they came around the side of the high school. The zombies had made it to where the closest elementary school bus had been, but now it was waiting for them at the intersection of the highway. The remaining kids were still clustered around the farthest bus, only twenty yards from the zombies, looking wide-eyed and terrified. There was only one adult with them. She looked just as scared as the kids.

James jumped out as they came to a stop next to the kids. The woman ushered them inside and James went around to the back of the bus. Fifty sets of undead legs were stumbling toward them in a frenzy. Aiming at the first one, he dropped it. Another fell in the front line from a suppressed shot behind him. He took out a few more, but they steadily kept coming. Behind them was an even larger horde of zombies.

"Let's go, kid!" Peter said from the driver's seat.

"Head north! I'll run to my truck!" James yelled at him.

The bus pulled forward and James ran alongside, heading toward his truck. A scream sounded to his left and the little dark-haired girl ran out of the school. She had blood on her and looked horrified. A female zombie stumbled after her, missing half its neck—the woman who'd gone in after the girl.

*She turned quickly!*

He stopped, shooting over the little girl and taking out the zombie chasing her. He ran in front of the second bus, scooped her up with his left arm, and took off running toward his truck.

He stopped dead in his tracks. Out of the side entrance they'd gone in earlier a steady stream of zombies approached the trucks behind his group. About a dozen had branched off toward him.

*They must have gotten in from another entrance!*

"Your six!" James yelled to his group.

Connor glanced over at the zombies and swung his AR around, taking out the nearest one, five yards away. The girls joined in, but still more poured out of the school. Blocked from getting to the trucks and with the last bus too far down the road, James looked around. Zombies were closing in from the west, north and northeast, so he did the only logical thing—he ran into the cornfield to the south of the road. The trucks started up, headlights shining into the night.

Entering the standing corn, he turned to the east, hoping the zombies would try following him instead of cutting him off. He planned to come out on the highway where hopefully his group would be waiting for him in the safety of the trucks.

The little girl clung to him fiercely. She had to weigh at least fifty pounds. Cornstalks whipped him in the face and he couldn't see more than a few feet. Tripping over something on the ground, he fell forward, twisting to land on his right side. Something popped in his side when he connected with a rock on the ground. He groaned, rolling onto his back. The little girl stood up next to him, unfazed, and began to tug on his arm.

"Come on," she said in a quiet voice.

"One second," James said, trying to catch his breath.

Pain shot up his side as he inhaled deeply. He closed his eyes and touched his ribs—definitely bruised, maybe even fractured. The girl screamed and he opened his eyes, instinctively raising his AR, but there was nothing near him.

The zombie was only three feet away from the girl, reaching for her, when a 5.56 bullet blew half its face off. The creature fell at her feet and she jumped back, moving next to James. He rose to a kneeling position, AR still aiming at the fallen zombie as pain flared in his side. Hearing more zombies groaning from the south and west, he picked the girl up on his uninjured left side, ignoring the pain. They needed to get out of there, and fast. Continuing through the cornfield, he came out on the far side with the highway a hundred yards in front of him. He jogged to the road, his side on fire. When he made it there, he looked back. Ten zombies were just coming out of the cornfield.

Setting the girl down, he brought the AR to his shoulder and took down the nearest zombie—grateful the gun didn't have enough recoil to hurt his side. He swung onto the next one, laser pointing at its head, and fired, spraying brains out of the back of its skull. The zombies only made it halfway before they were all lying dead on the ground. He lowered his AR and exchanged his partial magazine for a full one. Looking down at the girl, he smiled. She returned a weak smile, even though her blue eyes shone with fear.

"What's your name?" James asked.

"Olivia," she said, "but all my friends call me Olive."

"Hi, Olive. I'm James."

"Hi, James."

"Okay Olive, can you walk on your own and follow me?" She looked around nervously. "You can do it. I'll be right here."

"Okay," she said, grabbing his left pant leg.

"We'll go slow," he said. *For you and me.*

Though he still didn't think his ribs were broken, he also knew he was no doctor. They walked north on the highway, the cornfield blocking their view of the elementary school. When they made it to the intersection and he could see the school, his heart sank. The buses were gone and the parking lot his truck had been in was empty—save for all the zombies roaming around the schoolyard. There was no one at the intersection or anywhere on the highway that he could see. His group was gone, and he had no idea where they'd gone or if they even knew he was still alive.

# 3
# MISSING

James stood at the intersection, at a loss. Where had they gone? He flipped down his NVG optics and kicked himself for not doing so when he was running through the cornfield. If he'd done that, maybe he wouldn't have fallen, but that was a moot point now. He needed to figure out a plan before all the zombies wandering around caught sight of them. Instinctively saying a quick prayer for guidance, he started down the highway, heading north.

"Where is everyone?" Olive asked as she walked along beside him, clenching the fabric of his pants in a little fist.

"They had to get to safety," James said, "and we're going to meet up with them."

"Do you know where they are?"

*Nope.*

"Of course. They're just up ahead."

"Okay."

They went off the right side of the road into a small ditch in order to pass the elementary school and made it by without attracting the attention of any zombies. After half a mile, they reached an overpass going over the train tracks and took a break. His side was bothering him and he could tell

Olive was tiring quickly. If he wanted to move faster or get anywhere, he would either have to carry her or leave her. Neither was an option, so he slumped against the guardrail, resting his head back and closing his eyes. Olive came over and sat down next to him, resting her little head against his left side.

A warm feeling seeped into his heart. He smiled despite the situation. This was what it was all about. Even if he could save just one he would be content, but he had to help. It was his duty. He hadn't been able to save his parents—couldn't even do anything to help them. Now it was his place to help those in need. That was how he would honor their deaths.

At some point, exhaustion overtook him and he dozed off. Olive breathed peacefully next to him.

"Where the hell is he?" Connor said, throwing the radio on the dash. James hadn't answered.

He was going to kill his brother when he found him. How could he just run off like that, risking his life for complete strangers? Any one of them could betray them or even kill them, and then where would they be? Dead, that's where. But no, James's bleeding heart had made him run off *toward* the zombies to save people who didn't matter. There were only two people who mattered now—James and Tank. Emmett and the girls, maybe, but they weren't nearly as important as his brother and best friend.

"I don't know," Ana said from the passenger seat of James's truck. "He yelled a warning and I immediately turned to the zombies. I never saw where he went."

"I didn't see him either," Connor said desperately. "All I knew was all of a sudden the buses were gone and so was he!"

"Just calm down a little," Ana said.

She was fingering something at her neck beneath her shirt. It almost seemed like she was nervous or something, but he wasn't in a mental state to care. He had one thought on his mind and that was finding his brother. They drove north on the highway, following Emmett and trying to catch up to the buses.

"I'll radio them," Ana said after a few tense seconds. She picked up the radio from the dash. "You guys see where James was?"

"I think he hopped on a bus," Alexis said. "You guys didn't see him?"

"No," Ana responded.

"Dad doesn't know. He said he never saw him," Alexis said, sounding worried.

Connor cursed, his blood boiling. He knew that if he took the time to truly think about it, he'd find the anger was just covering his concern. But he didn't dig deeper. He was pissed and he'd stay pissed. Then when he found James, he'd punch him in his face and teach him a lesson.

*No, you won't because you know he's right.*

Connor took a deep breath, letting it out his nose. His brother was resourceful and tough. If anyone could make it, it'd be him.

"Tell Emmett to speed up. We need to catch those buses," Connor said.

Ana relayed the message through the radio and they topped out at eighty miles an hour. In five minutes, the buses were in sight. Emmett flashed his lights and they slowed to a stop. Connor drove up to the trailing bus. The blonde woman who'd been talking with his brother earlier opened the window.

"My brother, the man helping you load the kids? Is he with you?" Connor asked.

"No, he and Peter went to get one of the high school buses. They came back together, but I'm not sure where he went after that. Peter's driving the next bus. He should know."

Connor was pulling forward before she even finished, coming to a stop at the middle bus in the line.

"Is James with you?" Connor asked.

"No. He said he was going to run to his truck," Peter said. "Isn't he with you?"

Cursing, Connor wheeled the truck around. Driving down into the ditch, he righted it back on the highway, heading south. He slammed on the brakes when he was level with Emmett.

"Get these damn people somewhere safe," Connor said. "I'm going back for James; he's not on the buses. We'll meet you at the next intersection."

"Roger," Emmett said. "Ana, you good?"

"Oh yeah. He needs all the help he can get," Ana said.

"Okay, Connor, be careful," Emmett said. "If he's gone, you'll have to make the tough call, and you better bring Ana back safely."

"I will."

Pressing the gas pedal to the floor, Connor took off down the highway back toward Burns, a thousand worries eating at his mind.

*James walked into the barn. Inside, his father was standing with an arm around his mother. The barn was the cleanest building he'd ever seen, without a speck of dirt, dust or hay anywhere—and were his parents glowing? He could see their faces vividly, but how was that possible? They were dead.*

*He wondered if this was a dream.*

*Looking around, he shuddered. He recognized this barn. It was the same one they'd found their father in.*

*"Hello, honey," Diana Andderson said. Even her voice was perfectly clear, unlike in most of his dreams. The familiar combination of comforting strength brought back a flood of memories from his childhood.*

*"What is this?" James asked, a sob escaping his throat.*

*"What do you think it is, son?" Jack asked, that same look of unending determination and intensity in his eyes.*

*"I... I don't know," James said. "This has to be some kind of dream."*

*Tears freely flowed down his face and all the emotions he'd tried to contain burst forth. He fell to his knees, tears pooling on the spotless ground below him.*

*"It's alright, dear," his mother said.*

*"How can it be alright? This isn't real. You're dead. I saw you die with my own eyes!"*

*"Son, don't let your faith be shaken so easily," his father said.*

*"What?" James asked, looking up.*

*His parents were no longer there. Instead, a light so bright that he had to cover his eyes radiated from where they'd been. A feeling of absolute peace washed over him and his tears ceased.*

*"This is not the end," said an unfathomable voice.*

James bolted upright, startling Olive awake, who looked around with wide eyes. He hadn't even realized he'd fallen asleep. Blinking his eyes, he looked around also, shocked to be there. But why should he be? This was the same overpass north of Burns where he'd fallen asleep. So why did he feel like he'd just been somewhere else? He knew he'd had a dream, but he couldn't remember it.

*Well, it doesn't matter; a dream's a dream.*

His cheeks felt wet and he wiped them off.

*Was I crying? In my sleep?*

"Sorry. I didn't realize I'd fallen asleep," James said, standing up and stretching, flipping his NVGs up.

"It's okay," Olive said, standing up also and wiping the sleep from her eyes.

He felt refreshed and energized.

*That's odd. I couldn't have been asleep for that long.*

He looked at his watch hooked on a belt loop of his pants. It was 12:19 a.m. He'd only been asleep for twenty minutes. Yawning, he stretched again and it hit him. His ribs didn't hurt at all! Tentatively, he pushed on his right side. Nothing. It felt normal. He unzipped his tactical vest and lifted his shirt to examine his side, but there wasn't any bruising. The skin was red like it'd been irritated, but nothing looked wrong and it didn't hurt.

*I could've sworn I'd done more damage.*

Tucking his shirt back in and zipping up his vest, he looked around. If they were going to wait, this would be a good place. Or would Connor expect him to continue? No, his brother would come back for him as soon as he realized he wasn't on one of the buses.

"Wait it is, then," James said, sitting down on the guardrail.

Olive looked up at him curiously as she stood next to him and leaned against the rail.

"So, how old are you, Olive?"

"Eight."

"Wow! So you're practically twenty!"

"No," she said, giggling, "I'm only eight!"

"Oh, well that's pretty close to twenty, right?"

"No, it's like only half."

"Darn, must've gotten my numbers mixed up again."

She giggled and James looked down at her, allowing himself to see her for who she truly was— not just someone to save. Her dark hair and skin had splotches of dried blood, and even though she should be terrified at everything that was going on, she seemed reasonably calm. Where were her parents? He couldn't remember if he'd seen anyone with a family resemblance loading into the buses.

"Was that your school back there?" he asked.

"Yeah," Olive answered. "Do you still go to school?"

"Nah, I've been out of high school for a few years now. So have you lived in Burns your whole life?"

"No, I used to live in California with my mom."

"What brought you guys out here?"

"Just me." Sadness crept into her voice. "My mom died of cancer two years ago, so I came to stay with my aunt."

"I'm sorry to hear that. What about your dad?"

"He died when I was little. He was a police-man."

*No, wonder she's so tough. She knows all about death and hardships.*

"I'm sorry. You must be proud of your dad."

"Yeah, mom said he was a hero. I have a picture of them. You wanna see?"

"Of course."

He crouched down, his side still not bothering him. Maybe he'd just pulled something and resting had helped—a lot, but that still didn't explain why he felt such peace or why the pain of his parents' deaths had dulled considerably.

*Maybe the stress of all this is driving me crazy.* The thought made him smile. He'd always told people he was crazy. Maybe that was finally coming true. Olive dug around in a pocket on her jacket and pulled out a black coin purse with words stitched on it: For when I am weak, then I am strong. James recognized the quote. It was a Bible verse from either First or Second Corinthians.

"That's a cool bag," James said as she opened it, pulling out a worn picture and handing it to him.

"Thanks, I almost forgot it when we left. That's why I ran back in and Mary came after me…" She looked like she was about to cry.

"It's okay," James said, resting his hand on her shoulder. "There was nothing you could've done. A lot of bad things are happening these days, but we have to stay strong."

Silent tears slipped down her cheeks and she hugged him. He held her as she began to sob. After a little while, she released him and stepped back, wiping her eyes.

"Thanks," she said, sniffling.

"You're welcome. You know, you're a tough little girl to stay so strong. Are you sure you're not almost twenty?"

She giggled again. "No, I'm only eight!"

"I don't know…" James said as he smiled and looked down at the small picture in his hand. It showed a man and a pregnant woman, holding each other. The man was in a tan uniform with a California Highway Patrol badge on his sleeve, and he could see that Olive was the spitting image of her mother.

He handed the picture back to her. "Your parents look pretty awesome."

"Yeah, I don't remember much about my dad though."

"What else you got in that little bag?"

She opened it and showed him. There was a twenty dollar bill, a paperclip, a few hair ties, bobby pins, some loose change and a business card.

"Who's that?" James asked, pointing to the business card.

"That's my Aunt June. She works at the bank."

"Cool…" James said, his voice trailing off as a sound reached his ears.

He couldn't place it at first, but when he heard something over the constant ringing in his ears—due to all the gunfire and rock concerts over the years—he knew something was different. Listening for a few seconds, he looked to the north and noticed a light in the distance.

"Stay behind me," James said, situating himself in front of Olive.

He could clearly see the headlights now as the vehicle approached them on the highway. It was probably Connor.

*At least I hope it's him, but I better be prepared for the worst.*

He looked around for cover. It'd take too long for them to get to either end of the overpass and off the road. The vehicle was flying toward them at a dangerous speed. He readied himself, standing on the side of the overpass with Olive behind him and his AR to his shoulder.

It didn't take long before the vehicle reached them. As soon as the headlights shined on them, the vehicle slowed down and rolled to a stop a few yards away. James recognized the brush guard on the front end of his white RAM and relief spread through him as he lowered his AR. That relief quickly passed when Connor got out and James saw the look on his face.

*This isn't good. I don't think I've ever seen him this angry before.*

Connor walked over and stopped a few feet away from him, and James could tell his brother wanted to punch him.

*I've definitely never seen him this angry. I guess I deserve it though.*

"I'm sorry, brother," James said.

"You're damn right you are," Connor said. "Do you realize that you could've gotten yourself killed?"

"Yes, but—"

"And did you even once think what that would do to me when you were off saving the world?"

"I had to act Connor. I couldn't just stand there!"

"Then you should've said something and we both would've gone! Instead you did it alone and almost got yourself stranded *and* killed!"

"You didn't want to help them. How was I supposed to know you would go with me?"

"Because we're brothers, James, till we die. Remember? Through thick or thin, we stay *together*!"

James stood there, stunned. Why hadn't he asked his brother to come with him?

Connor continued. "And just because I said we *shouldn't* help them doesn't mean I didn't *want* to help them. I just knew it would be safer to leave and worry about our own!"

A single tear slipped from Connor's eye and suddenly James saw this for what it was. Connor was hurting—bad—and it came out as anger and overprotectiveness. He was just trying to cope with the deaths of their parents in his own way.

Without another word, James walked over and wrapped his arms around his brother in an unabashed hug. At first Connor stood stiffly, arms at his sides, trying to resist the urge to cry. Finally, to James's relief, his brother wrapped his arms around him and began to weep. It broke James's heart and he soon joined in. They stood on the overpass next to the truck, completely ignoring the world around them as all their pent-up emotions and grief came pouring out.

James didn't know how long they cried, but after a time there were no more tears and he looked into his brother's eyes. "I love you, brother," James said, "and I won't do something like that again."

"I love you, too," Connor responded, breaking the embrace. "Good, because the next time I *will* punch you."

"Fair enough," James said with a smile spreading on his face. He felt so much better now. Who knew a good cry could help so much? He couldn't think of the last time he'd cried like that.

Connor took a deep breath and wiped his eyes. They looked around, remembering they were exposed on an overpass only half a mile from a town full of flesh-eating monsters. Looking behind him, James didn't see Olive. His heartbeat increased and he looked around furiously.

"Don't worry," Ana said, coming over to them from the other side of the truck. "She's fast asleep inside. I didn't know how long you two would be."

James sighed. "Thanks."

"You picked quite the little one. She has a strength about her that's surprising for her age," Ana said.

"Yeah, she's been through a lot, long before all this happened."

"Now that *that's* over," Connor said, and James could tell by his tone that he was feeling better too, "we ready?"

"Let's do it," James said, going over to the driver's seat.

"Everybody buckled?" James asked when Connor and Ana had climbed in.

"You realize there's no one else on the road, right?" Ana asked.

"Oh, yeah," James said, turning the truck around. "Sorry, old habit."

After driving for a minute, James spoke up. "Aren't we missing something?"

"You're right," Connor responded. A few seconds later *Battle Born* by Five Finger Death Punch began to play over the speakers. "You know what? That's exactly what we are, bro. We're doing our best to fight and survive, to find a place in this new world. No matter the challenges we face, no matter how hard it gets, we aren't going to give up and we aren't going to surrender. Do you know why? Because we're freakin' battle born."

"Hell yeah we are, brother."

# 4
## DEJA VU

"This is where we left them," Connor said as they drove by the spot where the buses had stopped. "I told him to wait ahead."

"At the intersection of US-85," Ana added, looking at the atlas.

"Hopefully nothing happened," James said.

"I wouldn't worry about them," Ana said, putting the atlas away. "Emmett and Alexis can take care of themselves."

James nodded. "Yeah, I'm beginning to think Alexis was right. Maybe it'll be good to have you along."

"We told ya," Ana said with a smirk.

"The verdict's still out," Connor said light-heartedly. "I wouldn't be too smug."

"Oh, you'll see once we save your asses," Ana said.

James laughed and Connor smiled. It was good to see his brother smiling again. James was happy with how the night was turning out because it had forced them to open up—which was a rare occasion. He remembered the peace he'd felt when he awakened and was curious about what the dream had been. His ribs still weren't bothering him. He was conflicted. Had he really hurt himself as bad as he'd originally thought and then been miraculously healed? Or had it never been as bad as he thought and the sleep had been enough to relieve him of the pain? He wanted to believe he'd been healed, but the concept was so at odds with the rest of the world going to hell that he had trouble.

Arriving at the intersection where Highway 213 ended at US-85, he looked around.

"No buses and no Emmett," Connor said.

"They must've gone farther," James said. "Is there anywhere up ahead they might've stopped?"

"I'll check," Ana said.

James turned north onto US-85 and they continued on their way. The highway was less crowded with abandoned vehicles than the interstate had been.

Connor picked the radio up off the dash. "Emmett, do you copy?"

There was only static in response as he tried again, to no avail.

"Looks like there's a small town in about ten miles," Ana said. "The only thing after that is where we turn off for Chugwater."

"Let's get to the town then," James said. "They might've stopped there."

"What's her name?" Ana asked a few minutes later.

James glanced back at Ana, who was watching Olive, her small chest rising and falling as she slept peacefully.

"Olivia," James said, turning back to the road, astonished at the amount of protectiveness he already felt for the little girl. "But she goes by Olive."

"Cute nickname," Ana said. "She tell you much about herself?"

"A bit," James replied. "She lost her dad when she was young; he was a California Highway Patrol officer. Then her mom died of cancer a couple years back. She's been living in Burns with her aunt since."

"You weren't kidding. She's had it tough," Ana said.

James nodded, noticing a light on the east side of the road up ahead.

"That should be them," James said.

"We'd better play it safe and go in ready," Connor said, rolling down his window and sticking his AR out.

"Got it," James said. "I'll be ready to bolt."

Driving across a small bridge over a shallow stream, they approached the distinct lights of three school buses. They pulled off the road into the small town—with 'town' being a liberal use of the term. Meriden looked to be more like a collection of five or six buildings than an actual town. The buses were stopped in a line, with the engines still running. Pulling up to the back bus, James stopped as Emmett and Alexis walked up. He put the truck into park but left the engine running and climbed out to greet them.

"Welcome back," Emmett said, taking James's offered hand.

"I'm glad you're still alive," Alexis said, smiling warmly at him.

"Thanks," James said. "Me too."

"Good place to stop," Connor said. "Now, we ready to go?"

Emmett shook his head. "They want to stay here for the night, then head out in the morning."

"Of course they do," Connor said, looking to James. "What's the plan bro?"

James appreciated that his brother was giving him the lead on this, although at this moment he didn't want the responsibility. But he was the one who'd insisted on helping them, so it fell to him.

"We're supposed to meet Tank in the morning," James said, "but we can always catch up to him tomorrow afternoon. If they got out of a large city like Fort Collins, his group must know how to handle themselves. But these people? They're barely armed and don't even know what's going on."

Connor didn't look pleased with the idea. "Okay, I can see that. But if they continue to slow us down or put us in danger, we leave. I'm not abandoning Tank for these people."

"I agree," Ana said. "We owe them nothing."

James nodded. "Fair enough. What do you think Emmett?"

"I think that's a good plan," he said and then looked at his daughter. "But if they compromise us, we're gone. My daughter and Ana come first, period."

"Good," James said. "Then we'll stay here for the night. I'll go talk with Peter."

James walked toward the buses with Connor at his side.

"You didn't have to come along, bro," James said.

"Are you kidding me? I ain't letting you out of my sight again," Connor said with a smile.

James chuckled as he stopped at the middle bus.

"I'm glad you made it out. I'm Peter by the way," Peter said, sticking out his hand.

"James," he said, shaking Peter's hand. "So your people wanna stay here for the night?"

"Yeah, they'd feel much better with a good night's sleep and a little info on what we're facing," Peter said.

"We can give you the info," James said, "but first we need to clear out these buildings and get people situated. How many armed people do you have?"

"With guns? Only four. We have a few with some makeshift weapons."

"Okay, pull the buses around and have them ready to leave in case another horde comes through. We don't want to be trapped here. Then have your armed people set up a perimeter around the buses. We'll clear out the buildings and the surrounding area."

"I'll have them do that," Peter said. "And thank you, I know you're taking a risk helping us."

"This is a onetime deal," James said. "After tonight you'll have to clear them yourselves. We can only risk so much."

"That's understandable," Peter said, nodding.

"Good, then get those buses turned around and get the engines shut off."

James and his brother walked back to the truck as Peter yelled to the other drivers to get the buses turned around.

"We need to clear the buildings and the perimeter," James said to Emmett and the girls.

"I wouldn't trust them to clear the buildings anyway," Emmett said. "They'd likely all end up dead."

"That's what I was thinking," James said. "But you guys don't have to help. I only speak for my brother and I."

"Of course I'll help," Emmett said. "You girls can stay with the trucks—"

"Not a chance," Ana said. "I'm not going to sit and wait for you to do all the hard work."

"I'm going too," Alexis said. Emmett gave her a look, but she continued. "Dad, don't start being overprotective now because of what happened in Haven. I know you feel responsible, but we're a family and we have to stick together."

She touched her dad's arm, looking into his eyes.

*Those puppy-dog eyes again,* James thought. *They'll get ya every time.*

"Fine," Emmett said sternly. "But you two will be with me and *will* follow my lead."

"Yes, sir," Alexis said.

"Roger that," Ana said, winking at Connor, who shook his head.

"Gear up," Emmett said.

Everyone moved off.

James followed Connor to the bed of his truck where he opened the tailgate and pulled out an ammo container. They refilled their spent and partial AR magazines, the mindless act soothing them. Once they were done, James went to the backseat to check on Olive. She was still fast asleep. Peter had all the buses turned around and next to each other with the engines shut off. Armed men and some women were getting out of the buses and taking up positions around them.

*Good. Maybe they will adapt.*

Blondie hurried over to James. She looked to be in her mid-twenties and every bit a teacher with her blonde hair cut short, stylish glasses, and that look on her face that said he was in trouble for something he'd done in class.

"Did you get Olivia?" she asked with urgency.

"Yes, ma'am, I did," James responded, stepping aside so she could see into the backseat.

"Oh, thank God!" she said, pulling him into a relieved hug. She stepped back, smiling at him with tears in her hazel eyes.

*Well, she's quite enthusiastic,* he thought.

"Thanks for helping me with the kids earlier," Blondie said.

"No problem. Are you her aunt?" James asked, slightly uncomfortable.

"Goodness no. I'm Mila, her teacher," she said offering him a smile and her hand, which James shook.

"James. Do you know where her aunt is?" he asked. Connor came over to stand by them, having finished loading his magazines.

Mila looked pained. "Her Aunt June was in Cheyenne visiting family."

"Oh," James said. "Who was she staying with?"

"Mary, June's best friend," Mila said, looking sad. "She was the one who went into the school after Olivia. She didn't make it, did she?"

"No, she turned and I put her down," James said. "I'm sorry."

"So what exactly is going on?" Mila asked as Emmett and the girls walked up, completely decked out and ready to do some exterminating.

Before James could respond, Connor spoke up. "The world's goin' to hell, miss. You'd better prepare yourself now or it'll eat you up and spit you out—literally."

"We'll explain more later," James said, "but for now we have to go to work. Will you watch Olive?"

"Of course," Mila said. "I'll take her back to the buses."

"No need. Just stay here with her," James said. "It's safe and the buses are only a few yards away if you need help."

"Okay," Mila said. "Nice truck, by the way."

"Thanks," James said as he and Connor walked over to Emmett and the girls.

Emmett had traded in his cowboy hat for a black combat helmet with NVGs attached to the front. He carried his suppressed M4 and wore a black tactical plate-carrier vest complete with body armor and attachments full of magazines. Alexis held her suppressed SCAR-H rifle with a Trijicon VCOG scope, foregrip and flashlight. She wore a dark green tactical vest with extra magazines over her black jacket, and her suppressed Walther handgun rested in its holster on her thigh. Ana had a suppressed AK-74 with a Vortex holographic sight, foregrip and bayonet knife attached on the front. A coyote-tan tactical harness with her handgun and extra magazines was over top of her long-sleeved gray shirt. Both the girls wore black lightweight tactical helmets with NVGs mounted on the front and looked very capable.

*Alexis looks quite attractive, wouldn't you say?* a voice said in his head. He had to admit she did. With her hair pulled into a ponytail and a look of determination in her eyes, she carried her weapon with confidence. She glanced at him and he quickly looked away, realizing he had been staring. *Smooth James, real smooth.*

"Looks like you're ready to do some killin'," Connor said, eyeing the three of them.

"Damn right," Ana said.

James looked at her.

"What? Isn't that something you boys would say before a mission?"

"Damn right it is," Emmett said. "Time to move."

Emmett led the way past the buses and into what was more than likely the center of town—which was hard to tell because the town was so small.

"We'll go south," Emmett said. "You take north."

"Yes, sir," James said, moving off.

He took the lead and Connor followed. They backtracked a little toward a large house by the road. Approaching the front door, they flipped down their NVGs and Connor opened the door. James swept into a living room decorated with a couple of couches and a TV. There was a door leading off to the right and one across from the entrance. Checking the room, he saw no zombies, and everything looked relatively normal.

"Clear," James whispered as Connor came in behind him.

Moving with practiced ease, James made his way to the right and the doorway there. As they arrived at the door, they posted up. James swept into the room. It was a small bedroom with no threats inside. He left and they moved through the living room to the other door leading further into the house.

"Do you know what we need?" James whispered as they posted up at the doorway.

"What?" Connor asked as he opened the door.

Inside was a kitchen, with a dining room further in and two doors set on the far wall with a glass door to the right of those. A large pool of liquid covered the floor in the kitchen and two chairs were knocked over. Kneeling down, he examined the liquid. As his fingertips touched it, he abruptly drew them back. It was still wet. He stood up.

"Blood," James whispered, "and fresh. Stay frosty."

Connor chuckled softly, ruining the serious-ness of the moment. "Idiot."

"What?"

"You just wanted to say 'stay frosty.'"

James chuckled. "True."

"What were you going to say earlier?" Connor asked as they stepped around the pool of blood, moving deeper into the kitchen.

"Oh, yeah. That we need a couple battery-powered headsets like in all the movies."

"That's not a half bad idea."

"You seem surprised. I always have good ideas."

"Sometimes..." Connor trailed off as they drew near the side-by-side doors on the back wall.

One of the doors was shut while the other looked like it had been broken down. The glass door on the wall to the right was shattered. The shards of glass were covered in a dark liquid and there was a chunk of flesh hanging off the door to the bedroom. Proceeding with caution, James went to the bedroom while Connor kept an eye on the shattered glass door leading outside. James peeked in and almost lost his lunch. Inside, the remains of two bodies appeared to be gutted and all the entrails and blood had been tossed around the room. Swallowing hard, he made sure there was nothing living and stepped back before taking a deep breath. But even outside the bedroom, the stench of death was almost overwhelming.

"That bad?" Connor asked, still standing watch.

James didn't trust himself to open his mouth and respond, so he just nodded. Going to the closed door, he opened it quickly and stepped back. Inside was a similar bedroom to the first; however, this one was empty. He walked to his brother and they went out the broken glass door. Outside, James took another deep breath, enjoying the crisp night air in his lungs.

"Wow, that was bad," James said.

"How many are we dealing with?"

"No idea. All I know is they must've tried to get through every wall before they got out because there was blood *everywhere*."

"We need to get back to the buses," Connor said.

"Yeah, like now."

Turning to the right, they headed back to the buses in a quick but cautious walk. James came around the corner of the house and saw the buses. Everything looked normal. The few men and women were still standing guard. Walking to them, James noticed Peter and waved him over.

"What'd you find?" Peter asked, baseball bat in his hands.

"Not good. There are at least a few zombies roaming around," James said, "We thought they might come here."

"We haven't seen or heard anything," Peter said.

"Okay," James said, "We need to find 'em and kill 'em. Then we'll be back. Keep your eyes and ears open. You may hear 'em before you see 'em."

Peter nodded. "We will."

"Oh, and don't forget to aim for the head. It's the only way to put 'em down for good," Connor said as they were turning to leave.

"Got it," Peter said. "I'll tell the others."

*I didn't even think to tell them that. That could've been bad,* James thought.

Walking back down the dirt road to where they'd started, the brothers approached a long white building with five doors facing south. Outside the first door were a couple of post office drop boxes. James went up to the door and Connor opened it. Inside was a small, one-room post office with a counter splitting it in half.

"Clear," James said as he exited after checking the whole room.

They moved to the next door. It looked to be an apartment of sorts but was empty of blood, bodies or zombies. He moved in and checked the bathroom. It was clear as well. They moved down to the next one and repeated the process, clearing all the rooms in the building.

"Where're all the people?" James asked. "I know it's a small town, but still."

"They might've left before everything went down the drain," Connor said.

Going further north, they came to the next building and found a door on the far side. They entered, clearing the small, two-room house, then exited and stood outside, planning their next move. To the northwest was a small building, and farther to the north, sitting in the middle of a clump of trees, was a large house.

A gunshot split the night. From the same direction, another shot sounded. The brothers crouched down, trying to pinpoint the sound. The brothers stood there for a couple of seconds as the sporadic sounds of gunfire came from the large house to the north. A sound behind them made James turn, raising his AR. His laser rested on Emmett's chest as he ran up.

"Friendlies," Emmett said as he stopped next to them. The girls were a few steps behind him, doing a good job of covering his six and keeping their heads on a swivel.

"Gunshots," Connor said, "to the north in the big house."

"Roger, we heard those," Emmett said.

"What're you thinking?" James asked.

"Let's take a look," Emmett said, leading the way to the house.

James let the women go first, then he and Connor brought up the rear. As they got closer, a scream could be heard from the large house and Emmett picked up the pace. He went around to the front door, taking the steps two at a time. Moving up to the door, he put his shoulder against the wall. The girls stacked up on the other side. Connor, followed by James, came up to the doorway.

"May I?" Connor asked.

Emmett nodded. "You two take the lead. I'll follow and the girls will bring up the rear."

The door was open and Connor swept into the room with James at his heels. Inside was a large room with a door leading off to the left, a long hallway in front with rooms going off of both sides, and a dining room with an open doorway to the kitchen on the right. Connor looked right and James looked left. It was empty but looked more like what they'd come to expect. The table was tipped over, along with the chairs, and household items were scattered around the room. As they moved further into the room, James noticed the door to the left was open, with stairs leading down. He could hear scuffling and groaning coming from down there.

Emmett came in behind them, hearing the same thing. "Go, we got up here!"

The brother's didn't hesitate. Connor took the lead, heading for the stairs with James right behind him. Taking the steps two at a time, they quickly arrived at the bottom and emerged into a scene straight out of a horror movie. The basement was one large open room filled with at least two dozen zombies, but that wasn't the worst of it.

There was a family of four in the far corner. James watched, unable to help in time as the family was overrun by zombies. They went down fighting but were still torn to pieces without discretion— father, mother, and two sons. The similarities to their own family made the brothers freeze and stare in horror as their screams filled the room with a cacophony of pain. Their flesh was ripped from their bodies as the savage creatures descended on them in bloody fury.

The zombies in the back couldn't get at the fresh meal and instead turned toward the brothers. James was so shocked, so horrified, that he didn't even notice the zombies only a few feet away and closing in. He wasn't seeing the faces of some unknown family, but *his* family as the zombies tore them apart. *His* brother was there, twitching as a zombie ripped his intestines out. *His* mother screamed as teeth sank into her flesh and blood squirted from a gouge in *his* father's neck. And, in a moment of complete vertigo, he stared as a zombie tore the flesh from *his* cheek.

# 5
# PICKING UP THE PIECES

A suppressed gunshot made James jump as reality came crashing back in. Another shot sounded behind him. He watched as two zombies fell to the ground. Four more were in front of them, arms reaching, only feet away.

He didn't have enough time to bring his AR all the way up to his shoulder, so he began to rapidly shoot, aiming with the laser. He hit the kneecap of one of the zombies, causing it crash to the ground. His brother had recovered quicker and had one of the zombies down. Two shots behind him took down the last two zombies. He was finally able to get the AR to his shoulder and finish off the crippled one trying to claw its way to them. By now, more of the zombies were coming at them from the far corner, their insatiable hunger driving them for more.

"Upstairs!" James yelled.

He turned around, noticing Ana and Alexis standing a few steps up with their rifles at their shoulders, aiming at where the six zombies had just been. Connor turned and ran, following the girls as they sprinted up the stairs. James took one last look at the massacred family in the corner, then quickly followed.

*That's* not *us,* he thought.

Determination replaced shock and horror as he swore to himself that he wouldn't let anything like that happen to someone he loved. At the top of the stairs, Emmett was standing with his back to the doorway, keeping an eye on the rest of the house.

"It's a good thing we came down when we did," Ana said as all four made it to the top.

"What the hell was that?" Alexis asked, looking between the brothers.

"Later," James said. "For now, we have to take care of these." He motioned with his gun at the bottom of the stairs and the zombies that were beginning to climb.

James and Connor stood side-by-side in the doorway and took the zombies out as they tried in vain to climb the stairs. After a couple of minutes, there were so many bodies piled up that the rest of the zombies couldn't climb over them. The brothers had to move halfway down the stairs to be able to look farther into the basement and take out the remaining zombies. After killing them all, they climbed back up the stairs.

"Is it clear?" Emmett asked.

"Yeah," James said.

"Good. Time to get the rest of the house," Emmett said.

"You haven't yet?" James asked.

"No," Emmett said, "When we didn't hear any gunshots, I sent the girls down to check on you."

"Good call," James said. "Okay, let's finish this."

"I'll take the lead," Emmett said. "Connor, get the door. James, stay back and cover me as I go in. Girls, you got our six?"

"Yes, sir," Alexis said and Ana nodded.

"Moving out."

Emmett moved to the kitchen, Connor at his heels and James behind them. The girls kept their backs to the three men while keeping their eyes and guns on a swivel behind them. Emmett and Connor swept into the kitchen and James hung back, just outside the room. After clearing it, Emmett came back out. James stepped aside, waiting for Connor to pass, then picked up behind them.

In the hallway, two doors opened to the left while a single door led to the right, and at the end of the hall was a door to the backyard. Emmett cleared the first room on the left. James glanced in as he walked by. It was one of the sons' bedrooms. There were video game posters hanging on the walls. A feeling of déjà vu swept through him.

*I owned most of those posters too.*

He moved on, severely shaken. Emmett and Connor went into the room on the right. James stayed outside, covering the last door while the girls covered the way they'd come. The room Emmett and Connor were in was the master bedroom. There was a door on the far wall, leading to the bathroom. The room had a large bed and two makeshift beds on the floor with piles of food and other items scattered around.

When they finished with the room, the group moved onto the last one. This was the other son's bedroom and also looked oddly similar to Connor's, complete with a pet ball python.

"Clear," Emmett said, lowering his gun and exiting the room.

Connor stood in the middle of the room, looking dazed. The girls followed Emmett to the front room, but James walked in to stand next to his brother.

"Freaky, isn't it?" James asked.

"Freaky, doesn't even begin to describe it," Connor said.

"Did you... did you see *our* faces when..."

"Yeah," Connor said, looking at James in confusion. "You too?"

James nodded. "I think our minds are more strained than we think."

"I think you're right."

"But that wasn't us," James said, putting a hand on his brother's shoulder. "And that *wasn't* mom and dad."

"It might as well have been. We helped that family about as well as our own parents."

"We couldn't have done anything. Either time."

"If we hadn't stopped in Miles to get those damn suppressors... If we'd just shot everyone in the next town and moved on... If we could've driven faster—"

"Connor! We couldn't have done anything. If we'd arrived earlier, we might be dead too. Who's to say we would've seen the Red Xs coming and been more prepared? And what if we'd run into a group of them on the road? They would've opened fire before we had a chance."

"But we should've tried harder. We should've been there. Something… anything!"

"But we weren't and we're alive now. There has to be a reason. They wouldn't want us to lose ourselves or our faith because of their deaths."

"Our faith? What the hell got you so optimistic?"

"I don't know… a dream, maybe?"

"A dream? Are you kidding me?"

"No, but I can't remember. I just remember feeling at peace and now I *know*."

"Know what?"

"I still have my faith and God is *still* with us."

"With you maybe. He left me when he let our parents die," Connor said, walking over to the glass cage with the ball python.

James wanted to tell him about his ribs and that he thought he might've been healed, but the more he thought about it, the more he realized he didn't even know what to believe—about his ribs or the dream—so James let him be. He knew Connor was still struggling more than he was.

*Was it really a dream that made me so sure?* James thought. *How could that give me such peace and certainty?*

He felt his side. His ribs still didn't bother him. He wondered, once again, if he'd only pulled a muscle or done something worse. Had he been miraculously healed? Even with his faith restored— mostly—he still didn't know if he believed that. It *had* to have been just a pulled muscle or something. Didn't it?

"This takes me back," Connor said softly, staring down at the six-foot snake curled under a fake log.

The ball python was a gorgeous snake, with black and golden-brown markings running the length of its body. Taking off his tactical gloves and shoving them into a pocket, he removed the top of the cage. He slowly reached in, lifting the log. The snake looked up at him with dark eyes, testing the air with its forked tongue. Connor let his hand rest next to the snake on the wood-chip-covered ground. Then, gently, he picked it up. At first, it acted nervous, trying to slither away, but Connor let it move from one hand to the other. After a minute, the snake calmed down and was slowly slithering around in his hands.

"Just like Squeezer, eh?" James asked.

"Yeah," Connor said with a faraway look in his eyes. "Just like him."

James left his brother alone and looked around the room until he found extra wood chips and a small plastic travel cage.

"What're you doing?" Connor asked.

"We're taking Squeezer 2.0 with us," James said, putting the wood chips, plastic cage, heat lamp and other supplies into a backpack he found in the room.

"We can't just take him. Plus, who wants a pet snake at the end of the world?"

"Exactly." James smiled, throwing the backpack on and replacing the lid on the glass cage.

"How'd you plan to keep him alive?" Connor asked, still holding Squeezer.

"He'll probably die, but better for us to try than let him be eaten by zombies while stuck in a cage. You know you want to keep him."

"This is just so weird."

"Remember *Zombieland*?"

"Of course."

"Enjoy the little things."

Connor shook his head, but a small smile tugged at his lips. "Fine, but if it's too much work, I'll let him go."

"Fair enough," James said. "Now, I'm holding a cage that doesn't make a very good weapon. Cover me?"

"Of course, bro," Connor said, putting Squeezer around his neck and grabbing the AR that hung at his side. James went out the door first, feeling like an idiot as soon as he saw Emmett and the girls.

*How am I supposed to explain this one? Oh, hey guys, we're taking this snake because I feel like it might help Connor deal with the loss of our parents and make him remember the good times. It might be weird, but just accept it, okay?*

Luckily, nobody asked what he was doing, but they did look at him like he'd lost his mind—which he very well might have.

"You two are the weirdest people I've ever met," Ana said, shaking her head.

"What's the cage for?" Alexis asked.

"A ball python," James said, nodding to the snake looped around his brother's neck.

"What the—" Alexis began.

"You keep that damn thing away from me or I'll shoot it," Emmett said. "I *hate* snakes!"

"Oh, sweet!" Ana said, going over to get a closer look.

"Enough horsing around. We need to get back to the buses," Emmett said. "I'm ready for some shut eye."

"Yes, sir," James said. "That sounds great."

They moved out in the same formation as before. Squeezer was content to ride the whole time wrapped around Connor's neck and James knew the snake was drawing heat from contact with his brother's skin. Emmett and Connor cleared the last building while James waited outside with Alexis and Ana, taking a break from holding the cage.

"So what happened back there?" Alexis asked.

James didn't know how to explain. "It was… us."

"What?"

"There was a family of four in the basement, similar to *our* family. I saw… I saw our faces as the zombies tore into their flesh."

"Whoa, that's freaky," Ana said.

"Are you guys doing okay?" Alexis asked, concerned.

"Yeah… mostly… I think," James replied.

He had no idea what was going on or how to feel, constantly up and down like a rollercoaster. One moment he was able to forget all the horror and pain, and the next it all came crashing down on him. If it continued this way for much longer, it was going to break him.

"Very convincing," Ana said.

"A good night's rest will help," James said as he heard the guys coming out. He picked up the cage and could tell Alexis wanted to talk more, but she didn't say anything.

"Clear," Emmett said, exiting the building. "Let's head back."

They arrived at the buses without incident. James took the cage over to the backseat of his truck and noticed that Olive and Mila were gone. At first he began to stress but then realized they were probably just in a bus. Setting the cage in the back seat, he moved his rifle and the shotguns to the gun rack in the rear window. Then he moved the cage to the middle seat and buckled it in. *That should hold it.* Placing the backpack with the snake supplies on the floorboard in the middle seat, he walked over to where Peter was talking with Emmett.

"James, Peter was asking about the houses. Which ones are clear?" Emmett asked.

"I'd use the long building over there and those two small buildings. Leave the rest to sleep in the buses," James said.

"What about the bigger houses?" Peter asked. "I was hoping we could use those."

"I wouldn't sleep in them if I were you. They aren't secure," Emmett said.

"Do we know if anyone's been bitten?" James asked.

"I don't think so," Peter said. "That's how it happens, right?"

"Yes," James responded. "How about you gather everyone here and we can tell them what's going on."

"Okay, give me a few minutes," Peter said as he walked to the buses.

"You wanna tell 'em?" James asked Emmett.

"Nope. I'm not big on speeches."

*Great, I guess it's up to me then.*

"I'm gonna take Connor and the girls and gather all the weapons we can find," Emmett said, walking toward a large barn to the south of the road.

After a few minutes, Peter had all forty-three adults gathered together, the kids staying on the buses, and went to stand by James. "Everyone, this is James—one of the people who helped us escape."

"And almost killed us before that," Randy said from the crowd.

"Yes, we did," James said. "You'll understand why when I explain. The world has ended, or at least the world as we used to know it. Things have fallen into chaos. Even you can see that. The dead aren't staying dead, and don't even ask me how it's possible because I have no idea. But once someone is bitten—sometimes even if they die without being bitten—they come back. Zombies, is what we call 'em, but you can call 'em whatever you like. They don't think, they don't feel pain, and as far as we can tell, most of their bodies are dead. But the brain, that's the important part. It's what keeps them moving and gives them their hunger for flesh. Kill the brain and you kill the zombie. That's the only way. Any questions?"

"How smart are they?" Mila asked from the front of the crowd, watching him intently.

"Not intelligent at all, as far as I know. They can't open doors or form any sort of thought beyond their desire for food. They can see, but not very well. Their hearing is as good as ours, and noise will draw them. But their ability to smell is the best. Sometimes it's like they can even smell the blood pumping in our veins."

"How can their sense of smell be better than ours?" someone asked.

"I have no idea. It doesn't make much sense to me, but then again, I don't really care. I know how to kill 'em and how to survive. That's all that really matters. Anymore questions?"

He looked around and realized he held their full attention. He imagined what it must be like for them, learning the full horror of it for the first time, and he wondered how much they already knew from the news. No one spoke, so he continued.

"You'll have to learn these rules quickly or you'll die. Be prepared at *all* times. I don't care how safe you think you are. You never know what can happen. Stay quiet and make yourself as inconspicuous as possible at all times. Aim for the head and conserve ammo. Ammunition is in limited supply. You don't want to waste a bunch of shots if you can't drop your target. Close-range weapons are your friends. They allow you to take out zombies without wasting ammo or drawing more with loud gunshots. This works great with small groups of them or individuals in open spaces where you can see them coming. And finally, don't trust strangers. Even though zombies are bad, they're not nearly the worst. The worst part is the people. They're far more dangerous."

Before he could continue, someone spoke up in the crowd. "What do you mean 'the people'?"

"I mean everyone else out there. That's why we did what we did when we first met you. There are people out there that are..." he paused, struggling for the word, "... evil. They have no regard for human life and some even enjoy killing. I lost both my parents to a gang that used human blood to paint Xs on their clothing. The people are the worst. I'll say it again: don't trust anyone."

Everyone was silent after that.

"Okay, now that we know what to expect..." Peter's voice trailed off as Emmett and the group returned, carrying axes, scythes, shovels, pitch forks and other tools. Emmett dropped them on the ground in front of the crowd. Connor did the same.

"Arm yourselves," Emmett said. "And if you're caught without a weapon, find something to use or you'll die." He walked over to his truck and pulled it in front of the buses next to the road. This would allow him to escape quickly if zombies or people attacked during the night.

"Has anyone been bitten? What about the kids?" James asked, looking around the crowd. As a whole they looked relatively clean and uninjured.

Most people shook their heads and Peter spoke up. "I think we're good."

"We should check, just to be sure," James said, "This isn't something you want to take a chance with."

"You ain't checkin' us fer nuthin'!" Randy yelled from the crowd.

"Do you even understand what could happen here?" James asked. "If even one of you is bitten, it could spread to all of you!"

They didn't listen. Randy had stirred up the crowd and most of them decided it would be going too far.

"Fine, figure out who's getting the houses and who's staying in the buses," James said. "Then I'll come back and escort you."

Walking to his truck, he saw that Connor was putting Squeezer in the cage. He placed the lid on top and turned around to look at James.

"Nice having a pet, isn't it?" James asked, walking around to the driver's seat.

"Yeah, although it's still weird," Connor said, climbing into the passenger seat.

"But we've always been weird, brother."

"That is true."

James pulled his truck around next to Emmett's and walked back to the crowd with Connor at his side.

"You figure it out?" James asked Peter.

"Yeah. Those groups are going to the long building," Peter said, indicating a group of about fifty kids and twenty-five adults.

*Man, they're really going to shove 'em in there.*

"Follow me," Connor said, leading the people away to the post office apartment building.

"These two groups will take the other two houses," Peter said, indicating a cluster of thirty adults and children.

"What about them?" James asked, nodding toward the last group of people. While the rest of the crowd was filtering back to the buses, the group of three adults and fifteen kids stayed behind.

"They… want to sleep in the house over there," Peter said, pointing to the closest house with the broken glass door.

"That would be a horrible idea," James said. "Both of the bigger houses have *dead* in them."

"But you said you cleared them out," one of the women said.

"Yes, but that one has a sliding glass door that's broken, meaning anything could get in— rather easily, in fact. And the other has over two dozen bodies in the basement."

The other woman and man blanched, and the kids looked like they might start crying or run away—the ones that weren't currently asleep on their feet.

"So the house with the ones in the basement is more secure?" the lead woman asked.

"Did you not hear anything I just—"

"I know, I know," she said in a scolding teacher's voice. "It's not safe. But it's better than sleeping in a school bus."

*Not if you're dead,* he wanted to say but held himself back. He could tell that this elderly woman with her dark hair, stern features, and expensive clothing would not be persuaded.

"Then by all means, but leave the kids," James said.

"These are my students and, as such, are *my* responsibility," she said. "They go with me."

"But Sandy—" the other woman began. This woman was middle aged, with short brunette hair, homely features, and a round frame.

"They go with me. End of discussion, Margaret," Sandy said.

James wanted to punch her in the face and tell her how irresponsible she was being, but he held himself in check again. Though he knew this was an ignorant move, he also knew he was not in command of these people. They had to make their own choices and live with them. The house had *technically* been cleared, and it would probably be safe.

"Fine, but we're leaving, now," James said, irritated. In the end, nowhere was truly safe—not even the buses.

Connor approached him. "They're all settled in, locked and barricaded. I told them not to open the door unless they know it's one of us," he said.

"Good, take that group of ten to the house on the east side," James said. "I'm taking the other group to the small house and *her* group to the big house."

Connor looked at Sandy. James could tell he thought she was being just as foolish as he did. "Okay. Let's go kids."

The small group of two adults and eight kids left with his brother. James took the group of twenty to the small house and had them lock and barricade the doors. Then he took Sandy, the man, and fifteen kids to the big house. Margaret had wisely chosen to stay in a bus. He led them through the front door and took them to the bedrooms.

"These rooms are clear," James said. "Lock the doors and don't open them till we come to get you."

"Yeah, okay," Sandy said, taking the kids into the master bedroom.

Checking the back door to make sure it was locked, he moved toward the front of the house, realizing as he went that he couldn't force everyone to do what he wanted. He walked down and checked the basement, avoiding looking at the far corner, and made sure nothing was moving. Satisfied that everything was dead, he shut, locked, and barricaded the door. He left the house, locking the front door on his way out. He noticed Peter still standing there as he walked back to the buses.

"Everyone situated?" Peter asked as he walked up.

"Yeah. How many are we anyway?" James asked.

"A hundred and fifteen, well fourteen," Peter said.

"Why were there so many kids at the school?" James asked. "The outbreak happened on a Saturday in June."

"Vacation Bible School," Peter said.

"Ah, that makes sense. What about all the parents?"

"A lot of them use that weekend each year to do things without the kids at home. I know quite a few went into Cheyenne. They never came back. A few of the parents are here, the ones who stayed in Burns, but still, some never came after we got the announcement to stay indoors."

"You were there all weekend and half the week?"

"We were told help would come and not to leave for any reason. Earlier tonight was the first time we left to get some supplies from the high school."

"Wow, no wonder you have no idea what's going on."

Peter nodded and yawned.

"Tomorrow, we'll tell the kids enough to keep them safe," Peter said. "And, James, I don't think we can thank your group enough. You all saved a lot of lives today."

Peter stuck out his hand and James shook it. "Don't thank us yet. We aren't even close to safe."

"But we survived another day, and I'm beginning to realize how precious one more day can be."

"That's very true. Night, Peter."

"Goodnight, James."

James walked past the buses and Olive came out to meet him. "Can I sleep in your truck?" she asked sweetly.

"Of course, but did you check with Mila?" James asked.

"She said to ask you. Please?" She gave him her puppy-dog eyes. His heart melted.

"Sure, let's go."

"Yay!"

James looked in the bus window and saw Mila smiling at him and Olive. He nodded at her. She gave him a flirtatious wave, her smile growing. Suddenly aware of the suggestive twinkle in her eyes, he hurried off with Olive in tow. His brother was waiting for him at his truck.

"Well, that was quite a day," James said as he climbed into the driver's seat after moving the snake cage so Olive could lie down.

"Yeah," Connor said, leaning his seat back.

"What's in here?" Olive asked, looking at the cage.

"A ball python," Connor said.

"His name's Squeezer," James said.

"I love snakes!" she said, squealing with glee. "Can I hold him?"

"Not tonight," James said. "But you can tomorrow."

"Okay!"

"Goodnight, Olive," James said.

"Goodnight, James. Goodnight... what's your name?"

"Connor."

"Goodnight, Connor."

"Night."

James settled in, wondering where Tank was. He should've made it to the Montana border where they would be stopped for the night. Would he be angry that they were showing up late because they helped these people? Probably, but James knew that if it came right down to it, Tank would've done the same. While he may put on an angry, gruff façade, he was really a genuinely caring person underneath all the sarcasm.

James smiled, thinking of his best friend. It would be great to meet up with him tomorrow morning and have the Pack back together. Then they would be able to continue their way north and finally get to Alaska.

He glanced back, watching as Olive slept, using a couple of their coats for a pillow. Just looking at her made his heart feel full. He didn't know what would happen to them in the coming days or how many would actually survive, but he was glad they'd crossed paths with these people— especially little Olive.

"We saved a lot of lives today," James whispered to his brother, leaning back and closing his eyes.

"We'll see how long they last," Connor responded.

With that cheery thought, James drifted off to sleep.

# 6
# REGIME CHANGE

*Post-outbreak day six*

The morning brought with it screams of the dying.

James bolted upright, not sure if what he'd heard was a dream or reality. He looked out the window at the dawn light of an early summer morning. Fog blanketed the ground to the south of town where the small creek lay. The sun had just begun to peek over the barren hills in front of him. It was still chilly in the truck as the night released its hold, but it'd warm up quickly once the day began. He was about to rest his head back when he noticed his brother's eyes were open.

"Did you hear that?" James asked.

"I'm not—"

There it was again—a bone-piercing scream coming from the northeast.

"The big house!" James said, already grabbing his AR next to him. He quickly glanced back to see Olive still sleeping as he jumped out of the truck.

Running with all his speed, his brother right behind him, they arrived at the house to see the front door open. Emmett stood inside, M4 in his hands, looking down the hallway. Standing in the middle of the hall was the woman, Sandy, but she was no longer human. Fresh blood dripped from *its* fingers and covered *its* face. A small body lay on the floor at its feet. The brothers pulled up next to Emmett as the zombie started toward them. James raised his AR, but Emmett beat him to it as the creature's head jerked back with the sound of a suppressed gunshot. It fell to the ground, blood pooling from the hole in its head.

"What happened?" James asked.

"Not sure. Got here only a few seconds before you," Emmett said.

"Well, let's check it out," James said.

Emmett took the lead and the brothers followed. They arrived at the master bedroom. The door looked like it had been broken down. Fragments of it lay in the hall. Inside, blood covered everything—the floor, the beds and walls. Bodies—small bodies—were half-eaten and littered around the room. James couldn't help it this time. Bending down, he retched up the content of his stomach, which was only bile.

"That damn woman," James growled, spitting and wiping his mouth.

A sound down the hall made all three turn in a split second. Lumbering toward them was the man who'd come with Sandy, or at least what had once been a man. Now, he was just another zombie. James took aim and shot *it*. He noticed movement in the bottom of his scope and aimed lower. Out of the far room shambled the smallest zombie he'd ever seen.

*No! Not one of the—I can't think like that. It's a zombie, plain and simple.*

His brother made the choice for him by taking down the zombie. Another small zombie staggered around the corner and James sighted on it. Mercifully, he put a bullet in its head, ending the creature's miserable existence. Two more followed. They soon joined the others on the floor. James lowered his AR, a tear slipping down his cheek.

"I shouldn't have let them stay here," he whispered.

"There was nothing you could've done," Emmett said. "Just because we helped them doesn't mean we're responsible for them."

"Yes, but if I'd only—"

"Done what?" Emmett asked. "Forced them to stay in the buses?"

James started to speak but stopped. Emmett was right, but he still wished he'd done more.

When he didn't speak, Emmett continued, growing more intense. "I'm tired of watching you two stumble around with your emotions. I know it can be hard, but you need to get it together. You're going to get someone killed and I can't have you endangering my daughter. I will do what's necessary to protect her, no matter what you did for us. I will end *every* threat to her life without hesitation. Do you understand?"

"Yes, sir," they said.

"You have to learn to deal with the emotions on your own time. Because when you step onto the battlefield, all distractions must be tucked away. You have to focus on the mission and protecting your team. Our mission is to survive. We don't have the luxury of failing, because when we do it will cost someone their life. Remember that." He paused. The brothers nodded. "Good, now we need to check the rooms for survivors."

"Yes, sir," they both said again.

Emmett led the way into the master bedroom. "Anyone in here?" he called out.

No one answered, so they began to search. James and Connor checked each body to make sure they weren't going to come back, but most had been eaten to the point where they *couldn't*. A few of them looked like they'd been dragged from under the bed and slaughtered. With each body they checked, the sorrow and anger grew within James. The room was empty of any survivors, as was the bathroom. Moving out into the hallway, they went to the far bedroom. There was only blood inside. The people who had occupied the room were now corpses resting in the hall. Emmett and Connor went into the bedroom while James walked over to check the back door. It was the same as he'd left it the night before—shut tight and locked.

Emmett and Connor came out. They all moved to the last bedroom. The door was still shut and the room was empty.

*They must have just used the other two rooms.*

They went back into the front room. James walked over to the basement door. It was also still locked, just as he'd left it.

"That's weird," James said. "Was the front door still shut when you first got here?"

"Yes," Emmett said. "It was locked and I had to break in."

"The back and basement doors are just how I left them too. Were any of the windows broken in the bedrooms?" James asked.

After a brief pause, Connor answered. "No, they were all intact and closed."

"Someone must've been bitten," Emmett said.

"Probably Sandy," James said. "She was the one staying in the master bedroom. But it took so long for her to turn."

"Not necessarily," Emmett said. "Most of those bodies look like they'd been there for a couple hours."

"Why weren't there screams earlier?" James asked.

"The kids must've been so scared they didn't scream. Or they didn't wake up. Or we didn't hear them. The other zombies were fresh so she must've broken out of her room and bitten them recently. Those were the screams we heard," Emmett said.

"So those kids were locked in the room with her all night as she fed on them one by one?" James asked, horrified.

Emmett nodded.

James shook his head. *I should've insisted on checking everyone.* All those kids, dead, because of one foolish woman's decision. The sorrow within him waned as the anger grew. He wouldn't let this happen again.

"You couldn't have done anything," Connor said, looking at him.

"Yeah, I know," James said, clenching his teeth.

"Good," Connor said.

His brother was right. There was nothing he could've done, but that didn't change his rising anger. "Let's go tell the others," he said. *And change the rules.*

They left the house and all its horrors behind, but the memory would be burned into James's mind forever. On the way back, they stopped and informed the people in the small house that it was time to get up. Connor split off to collect the other groups.

Fifteen minutes later, all the adults and kids were gathered around the buses like the night before except they were missing seventeen. James looked to Emmett, but he shook his head.

"I asked last night if anyone had been bitten," James said. "I was ignored and lied to, and now seventeen are dead because of someone's poor choice."

"What happened?" Peter asked, walking over to him.

"Sandy and the kids are dead—massacred," James said harshly. "Because she didn't listen."

"No," Margaret said, covering her mouth.

"How?" Peter asked.

"Sandy had been bitten," James said, "but she hid it and turned last night. She slaughtered the rest of them."

"How do we know ya ain't the ones who did it?" Randy said, pointing a finger at him.

James was in no mood to argue with the ignorant man. "If I wanted you dead, we would've left you in the school, but we didn't. I endangered myself and my group to help you. Go look in the house. There'll be no doubt in your mind. Now, if you have a problem, step up or shut up."

Staring daggers at Randy, who was at the front of the crowd, James realized he might have to fight the man. He cherished the thought. After a few seconds, Randy looked away.

"Things are going to change now. I don't care who you are, *everyone* will be checked for bites and scratches or we will leave now and you can fend for yourselves," James said, Emmett and Connor standing on either side of him.

Everyone grumbled, but no one spoke up. James caught Mila's eye and motioned her over as Ana and Alexis came up from the back of the crowd.

"You three check the women and girls. We need to be thorough while still leaving everyone their dignity. Mainly check their legs, arms and necks. We can use the post office building. Let's get this over with and get out of here," James said.

"Oh, I'll be thorough," Ana said.

"What should we do if we find something?" Alexis asked.

"Let me know and we'll figure it out," James said.

Ana and Alexis walked to the apartment building, entering separate rooms.

"I trust you haven't been bitten?" James asked Mila.

"No, but you can check me if you like," she said with a wink and a smile, however the smile didn't reach her eyes. Before James could formulate a response, she walked off to the apartment building.

"We'll go set up in the other two rooms," Emmett said as he left.

"Make sure we get everyone, Romeo," Connor said, smiling as he walked after Emmett.

"Okay, everyone line up. Women and girls, the first three doors. Men and boys, the last two. Everyone must be checked or we'll leave you here."

"James," Peter said, "that's rather harsh."

James looked him dead in the eye. "If you want our help, it isn't given freely anymore."

"Fine," Peter said, "but these are my people."

"Suit yourself. But if I'm not happy with a decision, we walk. Now, let's go, people!"

Everyone milled over to the long building. James counted them as they passed. Ninety-four, not including Mila or Peter. They were missing one. *Oh, right.* Olive was still asleep in the back seat of his truck. Walking over, he opened the door and Olive sat up, rubbing her eyes and yawning.

"Morning, Olive," James said. "You want to come with me? Mila needs to check to make sure you don't have any booboos."

"You mean to make sure I haven't been bit?" she asked as she climbed out of the truck.

"Guess I can't get anything past you," James said, smiling.

"I like to listen to the adults. They say some funny things."

"That's for sure."

Together they walked to the long apartment building as people formed five lines outside the doors. James dropped Olive off at the line for Mila's room and stood back, watching as Peter came out of the far room, pulling his shirt on. He walked over and joined James.

"This is a lot to take in," Peter said, watching as people entered and exited the rooms.

"The sooner you get used to it, the easier it'll be," James said, watching a little boy about five years old standing in the back of Connor's line. His black hair contrasted with pale skin sheen with sweat. Wanting to check the kid himself, he held back, knowing Connor would get him. He needed to keep an eye out and make sure everyone was checked.

"You guys seem pretty prepared. What's your story?" Peter asked.

"Emmett spent years in the Marines. My brother and I have always been into the outdoors, hunting, and guns. Turns out that makes for a good combination to survive the end of the world."

"What about the girls? They seem to know how to handle themselves as well."

"Alexis is Emmett's daughter and he trained her well. I'm not sure about Ana. But mainly, they adapted quickly."

"I hope we can do the same."

"Me too."

Everyone was done but a little blonde girl, Margaret, and the pale boy he'd noticed earlier. Emmett came out of his room and joined them, along with Alexis. Soon, Ana and Mila walked out with Margaret and the little girl. The only one left was the black-haired boy. The door opened and Connor looked out. Finding James, he shook his head.

James cursed, going over to his brother. Connor stepped out and closed the door behind him. "How bad?"

"Bad," Connor said. "I'm surprised he hasn't turned yet."

"How did it happen?"

"I don't know. He just started crying and it took awhile before he'd show me his leg. It only had a small scratch on it, but it's bad now."

"What's going on?" Peter asked, coming over with Margaret.

"The boy's been bitten," James said, turning to them.

"Then we have to help him," Margaret said, trying to go in, but Connor blocked the way to the room.

"No one can go in. We don't know when he'll turn," James said as a crowd began to gather in front of them.

"You just want to leave him in there to die?" Margaret said, a little too loudly.

People in the crowd began to ask questions.

"What is it?"

"Who's bitten?"

"What do we do?"

"Just calm down everyone," Peter said. "No one's saying we're just going to leave him in there to die. Right?"

"No," Connor said and everyone looked relieved. "We have to put him down."

*Well, that riled them up,* Connor thought.

James looked over at him and Connor shrugged. It may not be the easiest option, but it was the best.

His brother spoke up. "Look," James said, "it may not be the easiest thing to accept, but he *will* turn, and if he's not contained, he *will* infect others. We either leave him here to die slowly and painfully, or we help him in the only way we can—"

"Which is to kill 'em?" Randy asked. "See, he wants us all dead, one by one!"

Connor had heard enough of the man. In a flash, he had his gun up and pointed at Randy's head. The crowd gasped and took a step back.

"If I wanted you dead, I'd kill you right where you stand," Connor said. He lowered his gun but continued to stare at Randy. "Don't take us helping you to mean we have to stay here and take this bullshit. You can decide on whatever your little heart desires, but if you want us to help, things are going to change."

Connor removed his gaze from Randy and looked around the crowd at all the scared and angry expressions on people's faces. Some of the kids were crying and cowering behind adults, and some just looked confused and oblivious to what was going on. Connor locked eyes with his brother and a look passed between them. James nodded.

"I'll make this simple," James said. "If you want our help and our protection, you'll follow our lead, plain and simple. If anyone has a problem with that, fine. Leave. But if you want us to continue to risk *our* lives for yours, then you'll have to compromise."

"Ain't no way I'mma go along with this," Randy said, growing irate.

"Then I'm sorry, Randy, but you'll have to leave," Peter said.

Connor looked at the man, shocked. *And here I thought Peter was a spineless coward, leading his people to death. Maybe he does have some balls after all.*

"But Peter," Margaret said, "they want to kill Henry."

"I know," Peter said, a sad expression on his face. "But if we'd listened to James last night, all those kids would still be alive. We have no idea what it takes to survive and we barely have anything that constitutes a weapon. What happens when we run across a group of men with guns who want to kill us? What do we do then?"

"We fight," Randy said.

"With what? The four guns we have?" Peter asked.

"They 'ave a whole pile of guns in the back of their truck," Randy said, a dangerous edge to his voice. "We take 'em."

Connor's trigger finger twitched. *If things continue like this, it'll get bad real quick*, he thought.

"Oh come on, Randy," Peter said. "Look around you. You want to get a lot of people killed? They helped us. Why do you hate them so much?"

Connor noticed Emmett slowly moving around to the side of the crowd so he'd be closer to Randy if things went down. With Randy so intent on the brothers standing in front of him, he didn't even notice Emmett moving at the edge of his peripheral vision.

"They ain't never wanted to help us!" Randy shouted furiously. "They just wanted to lure us out so they could kill us. There prolly ain't even a thing as zombies!"

"Randy," Peter said, voice growing hard. "Are you using again?"

Connor focused more closely on Randy's face, noticing for the first time that the man was shaking. His pupils were extremely dilated, almost blotting out the rest of his eyes, and his skin was covered in sweat. *He's on drugs!* Gripping his AR tighter, he watched the man closely, waiting for any sign that he needed to be put down.

"That's none of yer damn business! We don't need 'em. We can survive on our own!"

A couple of the men and women in the crowd nodded, but everyone seemed to take a step away from Randy. More kids began to cry, sensing the adults' anxiety.

"Randy, I'm only going to ask you once," Peter said. "Leave."

Something shifted in Randy's eyes. Before Connor could think about getting a shot off, Randy raised his M16 and fired. Emmett fired just after Randy and blood sprayed from Randy's chest. Connor also fired. The back of Randy's head blew off as he crumpled to the ground. Lowering his AR, he quickly looked to his brother, thinking James had been hit. James stood there, AR to his shoulder, looking at Randy on the ground. Connor couldn't see any blood or signs that James had been shot.

*But if he's not hit, did Randy miss?*

Peter, standing next to James, pulled his hand away from his chest. It was covered in blood. Peter looked down at his hand as his knees began to shake. James moved in as Peter fell, catching him and lowering him gently to the ground. Connor stood there, AR still on the crowd, making sure no one tried anything else.

"He shot me," Peter said, coughing up blood. "I didn't think he'd actually do it."

"All this stress breaks people," James said, putting pressure on the wound.

Alexis ran over to Peter, kneeling down to examine him. Ana stood at the back of the crowd, watching them with her rifle at her shoulder, and Emmett stood off to the side.

"Is anyone else going to try anything?" Connor asked, eyeing the crowd.

No one moved or said a word. He glanced down at his brother and Alexis trying to stem the flow of blood, but they knew it wouldn't help. Even if they had medical assistance, Peter wouldn't survive. Randy had shot him right in the heart.

"Take care of them."

Connor could barely hear Peter whisper to James.

"I will," James said as Peter breathed his last.

Alexis stood, taking a step back with a sad look on her face. James stood up, wiping the blood from his hands on Peter's pants. He shook his head, an angry light in his eyes.

*Oh, this ought to be good,* Connor thought.

"Last. Straw," James said, looking at the crowd. "No more." He looked to Connor. "Take care of the kid."

Connor nodded. Some in the crowd stirred, but no one said anything or made a move to stop him. Emmett still stood to the side of the crowd, M4 up and ready. He wasn't taking any chances either.

While Connor took no enjoyment in this—in fact, it pained him every time he had to do it—this had become his place. Actually, it had always been his place. Even when he was younger, he'd been the one to put down their family's dog. He'd always had a way of compartmentalizing things like that. In his heart, he knew he'd been born for war, to be a warrior. Opening the door to the room the sick kid was in, he entered, shutting it behind him.

They'd waited too long. The boy lay on the ground, convulsing in a pool of his own blood. Moving swiftly, he let his AR fall to his side as he withdrew his KA-BAR knife. Connor knelt. The kid was still alive and he could see the agony on his face. In a swift move, he plunged the blade of his knife into the nook where the skull joined with the spine. The boy died instantly, saved from a long, torturous death.

Connor closed his eyes and knelt, dealing with the emotions that rose up inside him—sorrow, pain, anger, guilt. Allowing himself to feel those emotions for a few brief seconds, he then pushed them back down and locked them up deep inside. They had no place in this world. He stood up, wiping the tears from his eyes, and took a sheet off the bed to wrap the boy's body in. Carrying the body to the door, he kicked it and a second later

James was there, opening the door. Without a word, his brother moved aside and placed his hand on Connor's shoulder as he walked out. Across from the building was a small patch of dirt.

*That'll work,* Connor thought.

The crowd watched as he moved across the road. Laying the body down, he looked back to see that James had gotten another sheet and covered Peter. Connor walked back and helped his brother as they lifted the body and laid it next to the boy's. They left Randy's body where it lay.

"Someone get two shovels," James said, not looking back at the crowd.

Connor watched as Mila moved first, followed by some of the other adults. The last few adults snapped out of their stupor, realizing there were still over fifty kids standing there with their mouths hanging open, fear in their eyes, and some with tears running down their cheeks. They began to usher the kids away to the buses. Two kids stayed—the girl Olive and an older boy. He looked to be of Hispanic descent, maybe ten years old, with long black hair and brown eyes. Emmett moved next to the brothers, watching the people return with shovels.

Ana and Alexis moved over to the two kids.

"You should go with the others," Alexis said.

"I want to stay with James," Olive said. "I've been to funerals before."

"I'm staying too," the boy said.

"What's your name?" Ana asked.

"Felix."

"Okay, Felix and Olive," Alexis said. "You can stay with us."

The girls and the two kids walked over as Mila and a man brought the shovels.

"What do you want us to do?" Mila asked, looking to James.

*And just like that, we're now responsible for over ninety people. Great,* Conner thought.

James looked around and then back at Mila. "Leave some of the armed adults with the kids in the buses. Have someone who knows about the buses pick the best two and move everything over to them. Gather up the rest of the adults, make sure they're all armed, and start gathering all the food, bedding, and other supplies we might need."

"Okay," Mila answered. "But what 'other supplies' *do* we need?"

"I'll go with them," Ana said.

"Yeah, I'll help too," Alexis offered.

"Good. Have everyone ready to leave in thirty minutes," James said. "If anyone has a problem, have them come to me. Those who don't want to come with us can take the other bus with a fair share of supplies. I'll even give them a couple guns."

"Guns?" Connor asked, looking at his brother skeptically.

"Better to have everyone who even wants to *think* of leaving gone now. It'll make it that much easier in the days to come."

Connor realized he had a good point. The people who wanted to leave would be more willing to do so if they were armed.

"I'll go tell them," Mila said, turning to leave.

"And Mila," James said as she turned around, "thanks. It's nice to have someone on our side."

She smiled at him. "You saved us, even risked your life for little Olivia here. A bad guy wouldn't do that." She turned and walked away.

"Ready?" James asked, handing him one of the two shovels.

"Let's get it done and get the hell out of this town," Connor said, plunging the shovel into the dirt.

# 7
## BACK IN THE SADDLE

The ground was soft and the brothers had the graves dug in fifteen minutes. They weren't six feet deep, but they'd work well enough. Looking down into the hole, James had trouble grasping this. Where had it all gone wrong? They'd saved a whole school of people and just like that they started dying, one after another. Why risk his life to save them in the first place if they were all going to end up dead?

"Did you take care of him?" Connor asked, motioning to Peter.

"Yeah," James said, "after I covered him so the kids didn't see."

"That was wise," Emmett said.

"What are we going to do with over ninety survivors?" James asked, looking at the other two.

"Well, they won't last long. Soon we'll have less," Connor said.

"Yeah, I know that," James said, defeated. "But even if they do make it, they can't go all the way to Alaska with us."

"No," Emmett said. "But maybe we can find a well-fortified town and let them find some semblance of a life."

"Do you think any of those still exist?" James asked.

"Yeah, you destroyed one," Emmett said. "Even though it was led by a psychopath, it was still a haven."

"That's true," James said. "Maybe we can get them somewhere safe."

"I wouldn't get too attached though," Emmett said. "It's hard enough protecting our own group, let alone two buses full of people."

"I'm going to keep Olive in my truck," James said, looking over to where Olive and Felix were sitting in the bucket of a bulldozer a few yards away, fiddling with something.

"I think that'd be smart," Emmett said, glancing over. "I'll give the other kid a ride. He seems like a good egg."

"Well, let's get on with it," Connor said.

They lowered the bodies of Peter and the little boy, Henry, into the graves. Olive came over and grabbed James's hand and Felix stood next to her. James looked down at the little girl by his side and was amazed once again by her bravery.

"We should say something," James said.

"By all means," Emmett said.

James thought for a second. "Peter was a good man, trying his best to protect those around him. He'll be remembered for paying the ultimate price so others could live. Let the boy find peace in you, God." Picking up some dirt from the pile, he let it drain into the grave.

"Ashes to ashes and dust to dust," Connor said, doing the same.

They buried the bodies and Emmett walked off to meet Ana and Alexis, who were returning from gathering supplies. Olive walked up to James and handed him a small cross she'd made out of two sticks tied together with bailing twine.

"That's perfect," James said, taking the small cross and sticking it into the grave of the boy.

Felix walked over and put a similar cross at the head of Peter's grave. James looked at the boy. *Emmett's right, he's a good kid.*

Mila walked up next to James and Connor, looking at the graves. "A good way to honor their memory."

"It's the best we can do in such a short time," James said, turning away from the graves and looking at the two loaded buses. He was stunned to find about a dozen adults and twenty kids by the third bus, looking his way.

"Those are most of the families," Mila said, looking sad. "I tried to talk them out of it, but…"

"You did all you could," James said, feeling an odd peace about it. He couldn't help those who didn't want to be helped, no matter how much he'd like to. Instead, he'd focus on the people who wanted help—the people he *could* help. "Let's send them on their way. Olive, take Felix over to the trucks and wait for us there, okay?"

"Okay," she said and the two ran off.

"They're oddly calm about all this," James said as the three of them walked over to the group that wanted to go their own way.

"They've both been through a lot," Mila said. "More than some of the adults, actually."

"So you wanna leave?" James asked, arriving at the group.

"Yes," said a hard-looking man standing in the front. "We're not going to take orders from some boy who thinks he knows everything."

"That's fine with me. I'll get you a couple guns and you can be on your way," James said.

"Good. Make it quick," the man said.

James smiled. "Right away, *sir*."

He walked over to his truck while Connor stayed to keep an eye on them. Digging around in the back, he pulled out a rifle, handgun, shotgun and a box of ammo for each. He walked back and handed them to the man.

"That's it? Randy said your whole bed was full of guns!" the man spat.

"It's either that or you'll be leaving at the end of *this* gun," Connor said, patting the AR he held.

"Pricks," the man said as he handed the guns out and the group loaded into the bus. "I hope I never see you murderers again."

"The feeling's mutual," James said, smiling sardonically at him. For a second, he was worried he might have to shoot the man, but then he moved off, calling them some colorful words under his breath. The bus pulled away and headed south, back toward Burns. "Well, good riddance."

"Less people to get us killed," Connor said, walking over to the truck.

"That leaves us with what? Sixty?" James asked Mila.

"Sixty-two, including Olive and Felix," she said.

"Those two will be with us. You have the rest divided evenly with adults and kids?"

"Yes. Greg is driving one bus and Bill the other."

"Good, and the food?"

"Split as evenly as possible."

"Perfect, I'm going to go talk to the drivers and give them radios."

"I'll be riding in Greg's bus if you need me." Giving him a smile, she sauntered her way to the far bus.

James walked over and met Connor halfway to the truck. His brother had already gotten a set of radios. "Channel seven will be ours and ten will be everyone's," he said.

"Sometimes I feel like we think on the same wavelength," James said.

"That's because we do."

"I'll go talk with them."

"I've got Olive in the truck. Felix is with Emmett," Connor said as he walked back to the truck.

"Good," James said and walked over to the first bus.

The man in the driver's seat was in his fifties, with short brown, graying hair, glasses, and a face that made him look even older.

"I'm James," James said, offering his hand.

The driver took his hand, shaking it. "Bill, nice to finally meet you," he said with a friendly smile.

"That's a relief. I thought everyone hated us," James said.

"No, they just don't know how to take all this, and frankly, neither do I. But I can see the good in what you're trying to do."

"Thanks." James handed him one of the radios and a charger. "We'll be on channel ten at all times while driving. Every driver will have one. If we need to stop, we do it as a group. One of the trucks will be leading. The other bringing up the rear."

"You're good at all this. What'd you do before?"

"Honestly? I was guide. I spent a lot of my time outdoors."

"Well, I'm glad to be in this group."

"Thanks, Bill," James said as he walked over to the other bus.

Greg was in his thirties with dark skin, a bald head, bushy black beard and tattoos covering both arms. He had to be over six feet tall, was broad at the shoulders, and looked like he should be a linebacker. The surprising part was that he wore the gray uniform of a janitor.

"Name's Greg," he said in a deep voice.

This was not the kind of man James had imagined. When he'd thought about strangling the man who'd started the bus early last night, he'd thought of a skinny, scared little man. Not this... giant of a man.

"James," he said, sticking out his hand.

Greg shook it. He had a strong grip. "So, you're the one in charge now?" Greg said, eyeing him.

"I am. We gonna have a problem?" James asked calmly.

"We'll see."

"Until we do, you follow my lead. Is that gonna work?"

Greg nodded.

"Good. Take these," James said, handing him a radio and charger. "We'll be on channel ten at all times when in the rigs. We'll coordinate our stops and stay in touch in case something happens. Follow behind either me or Emmett, whoever's in front, but keep a little distance in case we need to back out quickly."

"Okay."

"Good."

James was about to turn away when he caught sight of Mila sitting in the front row. She smiled at him and winked. James smiled back hesitantly, then turned away and headed to Emmett's truck. *What is up with that woman? Does she really... but no, she can't... could she?*

"What's the call, boss?" Emmett asked as James walked up.

"Boss?" James asked, taken aback.

"These people are following your lead now," Emmett said. "Regardless of your age you have their respect, and some, their fear. I'll follow your lead as long as it doesn't put us in undue danger. Just remember what I told you this morning. My daughter and Ana come first, always."

"Yes, sir," James said, glancing into the backseat at Alexis and Ana. He knew Emmett would do whatever it took to keep those two women safe. "I guess I'll lead then?"

"I'll bring up the rear," Emmett said, sticking out his hand. "Watch yourself up there."

"Yes, sir." James shook Emmett's hand and then walked to his truck, climbing in. "We ready?"

"Yeah, we're good," Connor said.

"Let's ride," Olive said, giving him a thumbs up with a broad smile on her face.

James laughed. "Did Connor tell you to say that?"

"Maybe..." she said as she glanced at his brother.

"Well, either way, let's ride," James said.

Pulling out onto the highway, he watched in his rearview mirror as the buses followed, with Emmett's black F-450 bringing up the rear. He couldn't help but smile a little. They'd lost quite a few since escaping the school, but they'd still been able to help them. Olive, Mila, Felix, Greg, Bill and all the others were part of his group now, and maybe they were all better off because of it. The responsibility weighed heavily on him, along with sorrow for the ones lost, but he had his brother by his side, the open road ahead, and, maybe, the hope of a new future.

"Have you called Tank yet?" James asked.

"I tried earlier, but there was no service," Connor said. "I'm hoping it's because we're in the middle of nowhere Wyoming and not because the towers went down."

"I guess we'll just have to try when we get to the interstate."

"That's what I was thinkin'."

Connor turned the music on and *Dead but Rising* by Volbeat began to play. When the chorus rolled around, the lyrics spoke to James. Was he going to be the chosen one or the fallen one? Was he going to be able to help those around him or fail them miserably? He was hoping for something along the lines of the former. Could someone do both? If so, he feared that's what he'd end up doing. He just hoped he'd be able to help more than he failed.

"Can I hold the snake?" Olive asked, looking at the cage belted into the middle seat.

"Sure," Connor said, looking back. "His name is Squeezer. Let me get him out and then I'll hand him to you."

"Okay!"

"Now remember," Connor said, after he had the snake in his hands, "don't move too fast and don't mess with his head. Just be calm and he will be too."

"Okay," she said, offering her hands. Connor handed her the snake. Her eyes lit up and her smiled widened. "He feels so cool! What kind of snake is he?"

"He's a ball python."

"And how do you know he's a boy?"

"You can tell by the tail. It's thick and tapers off quickly, meaning he's more than likely a male. It's hard to tell without a female to compare to," Connor said, turning back around to face the front.

Olive held the ball python up by her face and watched as he flicked his tongue in and out, tasting the air. "Why does he do that?"

"What?" Connor said, looking back.

"Stick his tongue out so much."

"Good question," Connor said. "He's tasting the air. Even though he has nostrils, he kind of smells the air with his tongue. It's a little more complicated than that, but that's a simple way to explain it."

"Makes sense," she said, nodding. Then she looked up at Connor curiously. "Why did you take him?"

"Because," he said, after a pause, "I used to have a snake a lot like him named Squeezer. This new Squeezer helps me remember my old life and what it used to be like. He helps me remember who I am."

"I'm glad he helps you."

She smiled at Connor and then went back to playing with Squeezer, putting the snake on her lap and watching him intently. Connor turned back and looked out the windshield.

*He probably didn't even know that himself until he said it. Good. Maybe something as simple as a snake will help him hold on and get through this,* James thought.

Connor looked over at James. "Thanks for making me grab the snake, bro."

"We needed a mascot to round out our little group… well, rather large group now," James said.

"Sometimes you know me better than I know myself."

"That's what brothers are for."

The white truck rolled to a stop on the small gap between the hills overlooking the town of Chugwater. James put the truck in park and grabbed the radio.

"Hang tight here. We're gonna scout out the town," James said into the radio.

"Roger that," came Emmett's response.

"Okay," Bill said.

"Got it," Greg said.

"We'll make it quick," James replied, turning the radio down and sticking it into his vest.

Climbing the small hill to the left of the road, James sat down on top, using his knees to support his elbows as he looked through his 10x42 Vortex binoculars. Connor lay next to him, looking down on the town with the ten-power scope on his .308 rifle. He couldn't see the town well, but he could see that a road on the south side met up with the interstate. If he wasn't mistaken, it looked like there was a gas station all by itself south of the interstate on that road. It'd be the perfect place to fill up and let the kids use the restroom. They'd have to play it safe and be fast, but they should be able to do it.

James noticed that one of the two vehicles parked next to the gas station pulled forward to a pump and two women got out. Three more people came out of the gas station and his whole plan fell apart.

"Survivors," Connor said.

"Yeah, but what kind? The ones we can help or the ones that need a bullet to chew on?"

"Can't tell from here."

"Well, this changes my plans."

# 8
# FRIEND OR FOE

So much had changed in the last couple of days. Alexis was still trying to process it all—the infected; her stepdad dying, then her mom; being on the road for days, then finally safe in a town—or so they'd thought. That "haven" had ended up being fake, a façade for something far worse than anything they'd faced on the road. She'd been shocked at the pure evil the priest had been capable of. How could someone sacrifice people to forgive a whole town of their sins? Not only did it not fit with what she knew of Christianity, but it made no logical sense. But Father Ahaz had done it anyway, convinced he was protecting his "flock."

Standing on the steps of the church about to be eaten alive by zombies had been a pivotal moment in her life. She'd known there was nothing she could've done and her father had been powerless to save her. In a moment of desperation, she'd done something she hadn't since her brother's death when she was a child. She'd prayed.

And it'd worked. James and Connor had rescued them.

She'd seen the pain in their eyes that night when they'd separately left Haven. It broke her heart even now thinking about it. There had been something familiar about them that reminded her of Mason, her younger brother. She'd known then and there that she had to help the brothers because she hadn't been able to help her own. She'd easily convinced Ana and her dad that they'd all be better off traveling together, and they'd set out after them.

Now they had a large group they were responsible for and that complicated things, but she was glad they'd found these people. Just since yesterday she'd seen a change in James. He'd risked his life to save a little girl and now he was the leader of the entire group from the school. She could tell the responsibility had already started to strengthen him and hopefully it would continue to do so.

The brothers were struggling with the loss of their parents, but she thought she could see that they were beginning to move on. She would continue to help them however she could. They'd saved her life and the lives of her new family, so she'd do her best to save them from themselves.

Alexis sat in the passenger seat of her dad's truck, her SCAR rifle resting between her knees. It was one of the many firearms James and Connor had collected on their way to Haven. Her dad had gone through the guns, and after taking the foregrip and flashlight off another, he'd set it up for her. He'd also found the rifle Ana was using. James and Connor hadn't minded sharing their "loot," as they'd called it when they'd stopped during that first afternoon together.

*Was that really just yesterday?*

It felt like days ago. Being on edge every moment, never sure when something might happen, made the days and nights drag on. She looked out the window, absently twirling her hair between two fingers. The fields passed by on both sides of the truck as the early morning sun continued to climb into the sky. It looked like it would be a hot day with only a few high clouds. They rolled to a stop after only being on the road for an hour.

"Hang tight here. We're going to scout out the town," James said over the radio.

Her dad picked up the radio. "Roger that."

"Okay," said one of the bus drivers.

"Got it," said the other bus driver.

"We'll make it quick," James replied.

Up ahead she watched as James and Connor ran up the side of a ridge and then sat down on a small point where they could see the town. She was amazed, not for the first time, at how well they worked as a team. It was like they'd been close for so long that they knew what the other would do without asking.

"Were you and Uncle Alex like them?" Alexis asked, looking over at her dad.

A sad smile spread on Emmett's face. He got a faraway look in his eyes. "Yes, honey, we were a lot like them actually. When we first joined the corps together, we were a force to be reckoned with, at least in our own eyes. Those first few years were the best I ever had in the military."

"What happened?" Ana asked, a sad look in her eyes.

She fingered something at her neck under her shirt, and Alexis wondered again what was hidden there. She'd seen Ana make that motion a few times before and still didn't know why. Was it a nervous tick or something more?

"IED," Emmett said. He seemed to realize everyone in the truck was hushed and looking at him. Composing himself, he looked back out the window at the hilltop. "But that was a long time ago."

"What's an IED?" Felix asked.

"Improvised explosive device. A bomb."

"Oh," Felix said, watching James and Connor.

"Do you have any siblings?" Alexis asked.

Felix shook his head. "It's just me. But Olive is like my little sister. I always took care of her at school."

"Well, you're part of our little family now," Alexis said, smiling at him.

She watched as the brothers sat on the point, talking and looking down into the small valley where the town sat. After a few minutes, they walked down the hill and started toward Emmett's truck.

"This doesn't look good," Emmett said.

James walked up to the driver's window. "We might have a problem."

"Let me guess, walking dead people?" Ana asked.

James looked back at her and smiled. "Always. But we have at least five survivors down at the gas station."

"Are they armed?" Emmett asked.

"Not sure," James said, "And there could be more. We saw at least two vehicles. Want us to go down alone and check 'em out?"

"Is there another gas station?" Emmett asked.

"Nope. It looks like that's the only one in town," James said.

"I think a show of force would be more appropriate then," Emmett said. "We have over thirty adults. They shouldn't have more than ten, if that."

"But none of our people are armed," James said.

"We can change that," Connor said.

James looked at him and smiled. "Brilliant idea, but we need to teach the ones who know nothing at least how to hold and aim a firearm."

"We'll help," Emmett said. "Girls?"

"Oh yeah," Ana said.

"Love to, *daddy*," Alexis said, smiling at her dad.

He glared back at her and she smiled wider.

*I think sometimes he really does hate it when I say that with other people around.* The thought made the moment all the better. He needed to be reminded that he didn't have to be serious all the time.

"Let's do it then," James said, hiding his smile as he walked back to his truck.

Emmett's glare faded as James and Connor walked away and she could tell he was hiding a smile. Her dad was finally starting to loosen his grip on her by asking her to help out. While a situation like this wasn't inherently dangerous, anything could happen. Thinking back to Haven, she knew it had to have been horrible seeing his daughter dragged away to be eaten alive, especially when he'd already lost his son years before. But he couldn't protect her for the rest of her life, however short it might be. She was her own woman and she was determined to prove she could handle herself— not only to her dad but to the rest of the group as well.

She climbed out of the truck, grabbing her SCAR on the way out. The rifle still felt a little odd to her because she wasn't used to the platform or the weight, but she was quickly adjusting and felt safer with it in her hands.

"This oughta be fun," Ana said as they walked to where James was ushering all the adults to the bed of his truck.

"Okay, listen up," James said. Alexis, Ana, Emmett and Connor stood by his side, and the rest of the people gathered around. "There are some survivors down there. Now, they may be friendly or they may not be. We won't know till we get there. We stand a better chance if we show them we're serious and don't give them the opportunity to attack."

"You mean we're going to shoot them before they shoot us?" asked one of the women.

"No," James said, "I mean we're going to give you guns and you're gonna stick them out the windows. It'll be a show of force and hopefully they won't want a fight. We're going to show you all how to use them, so those who've fired a gun before, please step forward."

Twenty men and women stepped toward him.

"Good, let's get started," James said.

"See what they've used and how much experience they have," Emmett said to Alexis as a woman walked up to her.

"Hi, I'm Alexis."

"Beverly," the woman said. She was in her forties with dyed blonde hair and a genuine smile.

"Nice to meet you. So you've used a gun before?"

"Yes, my husband used to hunt. I've shot a few of his rifles," Beverly said. "Oh, and his shotgun once, but I didn't like that."

Alexis turned to Connor, who was in the bed of the truck. "Beverly has used her husband's hunting rifles," she told him.

He nodded and began to rummage around. She hadn't noticed it before, but the bed of the truck was over half full of firearms. They had dozens of them.

"Is your husband here too?" Alexis asked, turning back to the woman.

She had a sad smile on her face. "Sorry, I should have said *ex*-husband. He left me two years ago."

"I'm sorry to hear that."

"It's fine; he was an odd man anyway."

Connor came over and handed a rifle to Alexis. "You familiar enough with this one?" he asked her.

She took the rifle and looked it over. It was one of her dad's favorite models—a Remington Model 700. "Yes, I know this one."

Connor nodded and went back to the bed of the truck, climbing in to retrieve a gun James had just shouted for. Connor handed his brother a rifle. James in turn gave it to Mila and began to show her how to use it.

The way Mila threw herself at James, with her coy smile and overly friendly demeanor, baffled Alexis. She never could understand that type of woman.

Alexis turned back to Beverly. "Does this look similar to the one you used?"

"Yes, actually."

"Good, then I'll just give you a refresher."

After fifteen minutes, they had all the twenty-eight adults armed with an assortment of rifles and shotguns. Fortunately, it seemed like most people had at least shot a firearm of some kind before, and the ones who hadn't seemed to be fairly competent. It was a good thing they were all from Wyoming.

James had most of the armed men and women sit on the left side of the bus, which would be the side facing the gas station, with their guns pointed out the windows. All the kids got on the ground on the other side just in case it turned into a fight.

"Good, we look quite threatening," James said, surveying the people on the bus. "Now, do not fire unless we're being shot at. If you haven't used a gun and don't feel safe, don't shoot. You could do more harm than good. If you know what you're doing, then do it. Remember, if it comes to shooting, it's life and death. If you don't kill them they *will* kill you, and once you're dead, they'll go into the buses and kill every single one of the children, or worse. If it comes to a fight, you need to remember the little kids you're protecting and do what must be done."

A few of them didn't look too happy about that, but Alexis saw some set their jaws. They would do what needed to be done to protect the children.

"Let's roll out," James said, walking back to his truck. Alexis followed her dad and Ana back to the truck and climbed in, rolling down her window to stick her rifle out.

They followed the buses down the hill and across the small creek into town. The highway they were on intersected with a road on the edge of town. Up ahead, Alexis could see the gas station on the left side of the road. A purple suburban and a red jeep were parked at the pumps with four people standing around them, watching the line of vehicles approach. They were all armed.

"When we stop, I'm going over with James and Connor," Emmett said. "I want you both to get out and stand where they can see you. Keep your guns ready but don't aim at them unless we do. If anyone starts shooting, put those people down, and if things go bad, get in the truck and get out. Got it?"

"Yes, sir," Ana said with no hint of sarcasm in her voice.

"Yes, dad," Alexis said.

"Felix, stay in the truck," Emmett said.

"Okay," Felix answered.

James went past the turnoff for the gas station and stopped on the road fifty yards away from the people at the pumps. The people didn't raise their guns, but they kept them ready. They were eyeing the buses full of armed survivors. Two more people came out of the gas station and stood by the door, looking a little shocked. That meant there were six people, three men and three women. All looked to be in their twenties, and they didn't *look* threatening.

*But neither did Levi,* Alexis thought.

James and Connor got out of the truck, leaving it running. Emmett did the same. The three of them walked over to the side of the road in front of the people. Alexis and Ana stood by the truck, watching the exchange from fifty yards away.

"Howdy," said one of the men. He was short and had pale skin. "Nice day, isn't it?"

"It is," James said, watching them.

*James is evaluating them,* Alexis noticed. *All three of them are.*

"Are you going to introduce yourselves?" one of the women asked, shifting uncomfortably.

She looked like one of the preppy types, the ones who cared more about what they looked like than who they actually were.

"Depends," Connor said.

"On?" asked the pale-skinned man.

"If you're going to start shooting or not," James said.

"We won't if you don't," Pale Skin said. "I don't think we'd come out on top."

"You wouldn't," Emmett said. "I can promise you that."

"Well then," Pale Skin said, "I'm Jeremy and these are my friends."

"James," James said, "This is my brother Connor, that's Emmett, and those are all our friends." He pointed back to the two school buses full of armed survivors.

"You got a lot of friends," Jeremy said, smiling. It looked like a genuine smile, but was it?

"Yep," Connor said.

"Well… are we gonna stand here all day or are you gonna get gas?" Jeremy asked.

"Gas would be good," James said. "Bill, Greg, pull those buses in and fill up. Girls, could you pull the trucks around to the pumps?"

"On it," Ana said, running up to James's truck.

Alexis got into her dad's truck. Greg and Bill pulled the buses around to the pumps as her dad, James and Connor walked through the ditch and over to Jeremy and his friends. The two people standing by the building walked over to their vehicles. Alexis drove behind Ana to the pumps. As she drove to one of the open pumps, she noticed her dad shaking Jeremy's hand.

Alexis climbed out of the truck with her rifle and began to fuel up.

"I'm Stacy," said the preppy girl with bleach-blonde hair and perfectly tanned skin.

"Alexis," she said, shaking Stacy's hand. She looked superficial, but her smile seemed genuine.

"We haven't seen this many people since we left three days ago," Stacy said. "We thought we might be the only ones left."

"No, there's still a few around," Alexis said.

"That's good to know," Stacy said, still smiling. "You hear of anywhere safe?"

"No, we found one town but… it wasn't safe at all."

"Too bad. We're hoping to find somewhere, but if not, we're going to Galveston, Texas. Spencer's family owns a big yacht down there. We'll be able to live away from all this and just come back to shore for food and stuff."

"Spencer is one of the guys with you?"

"Yeah, he's over there," she said and pointed to a tall, black-haired man.

Now that she looked closer, she realized all of them were dressed in expensive clothing and the jeep and suburban looked brand new. They didn't seem to be the snobby stereotype of wealthy people; they actually seemed like good people. This put her more on edge.

Levi had been one of the nicest, most genuine guys she'd ever met, and look how that had turned out. It hadn't really been his fault though. It was Father Ahaz, the psycho behind it all. Still, Levi had knowingly lured them into the trap, and even if he hadn't been the one in charge, he was a part of it.

James walked over to them, her dad and Connor following behind along with the other five strangers. "This is all of you then?" he asked, looking at Jeremy.

"Uh-huh, this is it," he said.

"Good," James said. "You guys mind hanging out here where we can keep an eye on you?"

"I thought we were past that." Jeremy said as Ana walked over, having filled up James's truck.

"We can't take any chances," James said. "We have a lot of children we're responsible for."

"Children?" Jeremy asked.

"I see the school buses, but..." Spencer said.

"They're there," James said. "We just had them get down in case there was shooting."

"Is it really so bad that people would kill kids?" Jeremy asked.

Alexis thought she noticed his eye twitch as he spoke. Was he lying? But why would he lie about something like that?

"It's a whole lot worse than you can imagine," Connor said.

"Wow," Stacy said. "It's good we met you first then."

"It is," James said, "So you don't mind hanging here while they take the kids in?"

"Not at all," Jeremy said. "We got what we needed and were just about to leave anyway."

"Thanks," James said. "Connor, Ana, you want to make sure the place is clear?"

Connor and Ana nodded and jogged off.

"It's good in there," Spencer said.

"But I understand you wanting to be safe," Jeremy said. "So, how many of those walkers have you been seein'?"

"A lot," Emmett said.

"I'd guess most of the population has turned," James said.

"Wow," Stacy said.

"Where are you heading?" James asked.

"South, as far as Texas if we have to," Jeremy said.

"My parents have a yacht down there that we're going to live on out in the ocean," Spencer said.

"Good idea," James said.

"If you can make it there," Emmett said.

"We started out in Texas," Alexis added.

"How was it?" Jeremy asked.

"It was one of the first places to go," Emmett said. "I'd say by now it's pretty bad."

"Oh," Jeremy sighed. "Anywhere else we could go?"

"North," Emmett said.

"We can't go back there," said one of the other women, nervously.

She was short and Alexis had barely noticed her standing there. It almost seemed like she didn't want the attention. The third woman was tall, with flawless dark skin, long red hair, and a stern expression on her face. The last person in the group was a heavyset man with small, beady eyes. Those three were a couple of feet from the rest and seemed like they wanted it that way. Alexis decided she needed to keep an eye on them.

"Bad?" James asked.

"Umm…" Jeremy hesitated. "We almost didn't make it through Casper." He added hastily.

"Anything we should know?" Emmett asked.

"Yeah," Jeremy said. "Where the interstate takes the big turn, there's a huge wreck, no way to get through it. We got off by the Events Center, but there were *a lot* of walkers there. We barely made it through."

"Any other way around?" James asked.

"Not that we could see," Jeremy said.

"But you guys might be fine," Spencer said. "That was the day before yesterday. They might have moved off."

"True," James said as Connor and Ana walked back out of the building and over to them.

"It's clear," Connor said.

"And there's a bunch of water and food we should get," Ana said.

"How are you going to pay for all that?" Stacy asked.

"Pay?" Connor asked and looked at her like she'd just grown a horn out of her forehead.

"Like with money," Stacy added.

"We've been leaving money for the stuff we take," Jeremy said, shrugging. "We didn't know how bad it was."

"Plus, it's the right thing to do," Stacy said.

Connor started laughing and walked off to the cab of James's truck. "Oh, we'll leave 'em something."

"Greg, Bill, you're clear to take the kids in. Make sure no one goes alone. Let's make this quick," James called out. "Once the kids are done, bring them back and have people start gathering up all the food and water and put it in the buses."

"Got it," Bill replied, turning back to the kids and adults in his bus.

Most of the group went into the gas station. A few stayed behind but got out of the bus to stretch. Mila came over to James's truck to get Olive, walking with her toward the station.

"Can I go?" Felix said from inside the truck behind Alexis.

"Oh, of course," Alexis said. "Just stick close to Mila."

"Okay," he responded, climbing out.

"There's a lot of little cuties," Stacy said.

"Like I said, we have a big group," James said.

"I'd say," Jeremy said.

"I think we should go," said the tall woman, looking across the road.

A dozen or so infected were shambling toward them from town. It wasn't nearly a horde and they were spread out, but it would still be a problem if they made it to the gas station.

"You see them?" Connor said, walking back over to them.

"Doesn't look like much," Spencer said.

"Watch," Connor said.

After watching for thirty seconds, Alexis understood the dilemma. Even though there weren't many, it seemed like they were gathering more as they approached, a horde beginning to form as they watched.

"We'll stay here and make sure none get through," Emmett said, giving James a look that indicated he would keep an eye on their 'new friends' as well.

"Well then, let's take 'em out," James said to his brother, moving past the pumps to get a clear view.

"All of them?" Stacy asked.

"Yep," Connor said, following his brother.

Alexis watched as James and Connor moved off, and she was glad they'd decided to follow these two. Though she'd been hoping to save them from themselves, she realized they may very well be the ones to save her again before all this was over.

# 9
## DISCOVERY

James hopped over the guardrail and walked over to the highway. Lying down on the side of the road, he flipped down his bipod and turned the power of his scope up to four. His brother joined him, lying down by his side.

"Just like prairie dogs, eh?" James said.

"Just like prairie dogs," Connor said and they both smiled.

James fired the first shot. The 5.56 bullet flew out of his barrel, arching through the air to collide with the head of a zombie two hundred yards out. The bullet, being a full metal jacket, punched right through the zombie's head, exiting out the back. The zombie collapsed face first on the lawn next to the rest area across the road.

"One down," James said, sighting in on his next target.

Connor fired. Another zombie bit the dust.

"Two down," Connor said, smiling.

With each shot fired, the brothers felt a little more at ease. This was something they knew, something they were good at. While they hadn't shot zombies until a few days ago, they'd put thousands of rounds through their ARs. There was something soothing about the recoil of the rifle, the muffled crack of the shot, the smell of gunpowder and the satisfaction of seeing the target hit—in this case the zombies' heads. They continued like this for a few minutes, taking out all the zombies that were within three hundred yards.

"I don't see any more close," James said after scanning for another target.

"I think we got 'em all," Connor said.

James rose to a kneeling position and looked around. There were a few zombies over five hundred yards out. While he would love to shoot them, he wasn't confident he would be able to hit them without shooting multiple times. He didn't want to waste the ammo. His brother stood up next to him. They walked back to the people standing around the pumps.

"Wow," Stacy said, "I guess you're good at that."

"Yes, miss, we are," Connor said.

James smiled. It felt so good to let go of everything and just focus on taking down targets. With the zombies moving slowly and being so spread out, it'd been easy shooting. He'd had plenty of time to sight in on a head and gently squeeze the trigger. When he'd first heard of the outbreak, he thought that's what it was going to be like—picking off easy shots with plenty of time to aim, but he'd quickly learned it was usually nothing like that.

"Feel better?" Alexis asked, looking at him with a slight smile.

"Actually," James said, "it felt great to forget the chaos for a bit."

"Wish I could've joined you," Emmett said.

"Then there would've been nothin' for us to shoot!" James said.

Emmett chuckled. "I'm not that good."

"Don't be deceived by his humility," Ana said. "I've seen him pull off some hellacious shots, especially with his handgun."

"See, that's where you have us beat, hands down," Connor said.

"Handguns are tough," Emmett said. "Takes a lot of practice, and I've had a lot."

James watched as the adults from their group began to bring out bags of food and cases of water and stack them in the back of the buses. They'd be sitting good for a while. He knew stocking now would mean a world of difference later. The more time that passed, the more scarce supplies would become.

"I think we're gonna head out," Jeremy said.

"Well, it was good talkin' with you," James said, sticking his hand out.

Jeremy shook it. "Likewise, and thanks for the advice. We'll make sure to watch our backs. And you… be careful up north."

"We will," James said.

Stacy and Spencer waved goodbye as they loaded into the suburban with Jeremy and the three silent ones piled into the jeep. Both vehicles pulled out and turned south on the interstate. Before long, they were out of sight.

"That was refreshing," Ana said. "They didn't shoot at us, threaten us, or kill us."

"Those types of people are becoming rare for a reason," Emmett said.

"They're soft," Connor said.

"Yeah, but at least they aren't losing their humanity," James said.

"And we are?" Connor asked, faking hurt.

"There for a second…" James said.

"It's easy to do from time to time," Emmett said. "Trust me."

The conversation died. Ana and Connor moved off to help load supplies while the three of them moved out to the road to keep watch. Fifteen minutes and a few more rounds from their rifles later, they were ready to go. Pulling out onto I-25, James turned north. He looked in his rearview mirror and was happy to see both buses were following, with Emmett bringing up the rear. Another stop and they were still alive.

"We need to call Tank now that we have service," James said.

"I did earlier. It went straight to voicemail," Connor said.

"He must've let his battery run down," James said. He was worried it might be something worse, but he wouldn't let himself think like that until he knew for sure.

"Yeah, I'll try again later," Connor said.

"Can I move Squeezer and lay down?" Olive asked, yawning.

"Of course," James said.

Connor moved the cage over, allowing Olive to lie down on the seat.

"Better?" Connor asked.

"Yeah, thanks," Olive said as she balled up both of their jackets and laid her head on them.

Soon, her breathing had slowed and she lay peacefully, like a little angel. Looking at her, James felt an intense desire to protect her at all costs. She didn't feel like a stranger but rather someone close to him, like a sister, and he figured that strong feelings must grow under the stress of life-and-death situations. He'd never grown so attached to people so easily before all this happened, and now here he was, thinking of Olive and Ana as sisters, Emmett as a father and Alexis as… what *did* he feel for her? It confused him and he decided not to dwell on it. He'd only known her for two days now. The sleigh scene from *Frozen* played in his head, with Anna and Kristoff arguing about falling in love in a single day.

He laughed out loud and Connor looked at him. "You goin' crazy, bro?" he asked.

"No, just thinkin'," James said.

"About?" Connor asked.

"You know the sleigh scene in *Frozen* when… actually never mind."

"James, not again."

"What?"

"Alexis, isn't it? Or is it that Mila girl? She really seems into you."

"I don't know what I'm feeling."

"You're crushing. You've always crushed quickly."

"I have not."

"Really? What about Liz, Vanessa, Emily, Cortana, Arwen—"

"Those last two aren't even real people!"

"But you still crushed on them."

"I was in middle school! That's normal."

"You've never been normal, bro."

"Just shut up. You missed the whole point."

"Oh, I think I got it," Connor said, smiling.

James stared out the windshield, wanting to be mad at his brother, but he couldn't. Connor was just ribbing him, and while he hated it, there was some truth to it.

*So maybe I have liked girls quickly before,* James thought, *but never this quickly! I still think the apocalypse is to blame.*

James turned the stereo on and *The Last One Alive* by Demon Hunter played through the speakers. He sighed and focused on the road in front of him. Maybe this would all work out somehow. As he drove north on I-25, he prayed. It was a simple prayer for protection and guidance—and hope.

The hot afternoon sun was at its peak when they drove into the outskirts of Casper.

"Stay frosty," Connor said into the radio.

"We'll let you know if we see anything," Alexis said.

"Be looking for the Events Center exit," James said.

Connor nodded. "I'll be watching for that and a whole lot more."

Olive was now awake and sitting up in the backseat, holding Squeezer. She'd grown attached to the snake already and would sit and hold him for hours.

"Olive, you want to put the snake away?" James asked. "We need to be ready for the worst up here."

"Yep," she said, gently laying the ball python back in the cage and securing the lid.

"Zombies or people?" she asked.

"What?" James asked, glancing back at her.

"Who you're worried about."

"Both," Connor said.

"But, I hope we don't have to worry about either," James said.

They continued through town, having to slow with all the obstacles. Fortunately, there was a clear path all the way into town. In some places it looked like something had rammed vehicles off the road to make a way through the mess.

"We're approaching the Events Center exit," Connor said, looking up ahead. "I can see a lot of zombies hanging around that exit. It doesn't look good."

"Can you see the corner where the wreck is?" James asked. He was having a strange feeling to continue on the interstate. He absently felt at his ribs. They still didn't hurt and he was beginning to believe he'd been healed. He recognized the feeling he was having now and decided he would trust it.

"I can see a lot of vehicles up there, but I can't tell if we can get through or not."

"Radio the rest. Tell them to hang tight at the exit. If we get stuck, have them go on."

Connor picked up the radio and repeated the instructions.

"You sure?" Ana asked over the radio. "Jeremy said it was blocked."

"Yes, trust me," James said. "I have a feeling."

"Oh great," Connor muttered before answering Ana. "We're going on. Be ready to hightail it."

"Roger," she said in a serious tone. "Dammit, now you have me saying it."

Connor chuckled. "Be careful or we'll have you saying 'sir' or 'ma'am' every time you address someone."

"I draw the line there."

As they continued and got a better look at the Events Center in the distance, they could see zombies all over the place. They weren't just at the exit but all around it, like they'd been drawn there at some point. Approaching the turn in the interstate, James noticed the huge wreck Jeremy had talked about and his heart sank. If he was wrong, they'd have to turn around and some of the closer zombies were already starting to stumble toward them. The overpass loomed ahead, with cars spread out all around it, but in the middle of the pile there was a path.

"Just as I thought!" James exclaimed. "Get 'em up here. We're good to go."

"Bring it up," Connor said into the radio. "Looks like someone punched through the wreck."

"Headed your way," Ana said.

"You saw it too?" James asked his brother.

"Hard to miss," Connor said. "I'm just glad they came through here. Whatever's doing it has some serious power to push all these vehicles out of the way."

"What's hard to miss?" Olive asked.

"Someone has been pushing vehicles out of the way to clear a path," James said.

"I know," Olive said smugly.

"How do you know?" Connor asked.

"I've been praying we'd get through," Olive said.

"Well, it worked," James said. "Keep up those prayers."

"I will," she said, smiling.

"If we can keep this pace, we only have maybe five or six more hours to the Montana border," James said. "We should get there tonight, no problem."

"I'll try Tank again," Connor said, pulling his phone out of his pocket.

"Hopefully he has it charged now," James said, dreading the alternative.

Connor put the phone to his ear. A few seconds later he pulled it back and looked at it. His face fell.

*Not now,* James thought.

"No service," Connor said.

"Damn," James muttered.

"Hey, mister," Olive said from the backseat.

"Sorry," James said. "See if someone in Emmett's truck can get service."

"You guys have any cell service?" Connor asked through the radio.

A minute later. "Nothing," Ana said. "Does that mean what I think it does?"

"Yep, the cell towers are down," Connor said.

"Great," Ana said.

"We'll just have to wait and see if he's at the border," James said. "He'll know about it and start leaving signs if they moved on."

"My guess is they'd wait a day," Connor said. "Wait!"

"What?"

"We have SAT phones in the back!"

"Duh," James said, just realizing it too. They had four satellite phones in the bed of the truck they used when they went off the grid, hunting for weeks at a time. "They won't help us now, but they'll be good for future use."

"Ana," Connor said over the radio.

"What now?"

"Good news. Remind us to give you a SAT phone when we stop next."

"You just remembered those?"

"Yep."

"Good thinking. We'll remind you. Now leave us alone. We're having an interesting conversation."

"About?" Connor asked, unusually curious.

"Santa Claus," she answered, and James could hear the smile in her voice.

"I bet." Connor put the radio back on the dash. "Is it just me, or is she one of the weirdest women ever?"

"Not just you. She's an odd duck."

"I like her," Olive said.

"Of course, you would," James said. "You're just as odd!"

"Good! I like being different."

All three laughed.

"That's not a bad thing," James said, smiling back at her.

"I know," she said, smiling too.

They continued north of Casper, cutting their way through the sagebrush flats. Medium-sized white and burnt-orange animals grazed on the sides of the interstate, black horns sprouting from their heads.

"Antelope!" Olive said excitedly.

"They sure are," James said, eyeing them admiringly. "Look at that buck! He's huge! Imagine how big he'll be when his horns are done growing and hunting season rolls around."

"That is a nice buck," Connor agreed.

"There's so many of them," Olive said with a smile. "I loved watching the ones at home. They're so pretty."

"Olive, look there," James said, pointing to a doe and a young fawn.

"Is that a baby?"

"It is."

"He's so cute!"

"Did you know they're the only horned animals to drop their horns like antlered animals do?" James asked Olive.

"No."

"Yep. See, most horned animals, like sheep and goats, continue growing their horns year after year while antlered animals, like elk and deer, drop their antlers every year and have to grow them back in the summer. But antelope drop their horns every year and grow them back."

"That's cool. So antelope are special?"

"Exactly."

"Good, because they're my favorite animal."

"Good choice," James said, smiling back at her.

Olive looked out the window and then back at James, a worried look on her face. "Won't the zombies eat them too?"

"If they can catch 'em," James said. "Antelope are one of the fastest animals, second only to a cheetah, and they can run up to fifty-five miles an hour. They also have great eyesight, allowing them to see predators coming from miles away, and like most herbivores, they're easily spooked and won't let a predator get anywhere near them if they can help it. I'm guessing that most animals like them will be safe from zombies."

"How do you guys know so much about animals?" she asked.

"We're both hunters and I guided for a job. You learn a lot about the animals you hunt, and you grow to respect and admire them."

"That," Connor said, "and a lot of *Animal Planet*."

"I love animals. Tell me more!"

"Do you know the only two mammals that lay eggs?" James asked.

They passed the herd of antelope that continued to graze like nothing had changed and the world wasn't ending.

They'd stopped at a secluded gas station on the west side of Kaycee, where they'd fueled up and the kids had used the restroom. Now they were north of Buffalo and making great time, the evening sun sinking in the sky. The same vehicle that'd cleared a path through Casper had been this way and there was a clear route wide enough for the buses. A few zombies wandered around. James and Connor made sure to clear them out before the buses came through. The last thing they needed was one of the buses running over a corpse and getting a flat tire.

All afternoon James had been wondering where Tank was and whether he'd waited or continued on. A few times he even found himself questioning if they should've rescued all these people, but when those doubts arose, all he had to do was look back at Olive and realize it was well worth it.

"What's that?" Connor said.

James looked ahead to where his brother was pointing and noticed a pile of cars across the interstate.

"Ah, sh—" James started to say but cut himself off, glancing back at Olive.

The truck rolled to a stop and he pulled his binoculars off the dash. The interstate was at a slight incline and ahead there was a gentle right turn. Before the turn, about two hundred yards away, was a bunch of abandoned vehicles stretching across both lanes of the interstate. It didn't look like it'd been a wreck and there were no other vehicles in sight. They'd have to go around.

"Does this smell fishy to you?" James asked.

"Could be a trap," Connor said. "We should check it out."

"Agreed," James said.

"Should I stay here?" Olive asked.

"Yes," James said as he picked up the radio and spoke, turning it to channel seven. "Emmett, you copy?"

"Roger," he said. "What do you have?"

"A roadblock. Might be a trap. We're gonna check it out. Would you come up and drive? That way, if need be you can hightail it outta here."

"I'll be up," Emmett said.

"Be safe," Olive said as James opened the door.

He smiled back at her. "We will."

James climbed out of the truck, outfitted in his tactical vest and AR in his hands. Similarly armed, Connor walked around the front to join him as Emmett walked from the back of the caravan. He had his M4 in his hands.

"That could definitely be a barricade," Emmett said, eyeing it.

"That's what we thought. Won't hurt to go take a look," James said.

"We'll stay back and wait for your signal. If we have to take off, we'll go around to the west on US-87. Meet us there."

"Sounds good," James said.

The brothers walked up to the collection of vehicles, scanning all around them. There was a hill to the east of the barricade that would make a good place to stage an ambush. They paid special attention to that. As they approached the barricade, they noticed three vehicles in a line, looking like they'd been heading north. They didn't seem to be a part of the barricade. Reaching the first vehicle in the back—a tan minivan—they saw the first zombie. It was inside the minivan, smacking on the glass to get out. They left it, continuing on.

"Bro," James said, "Look at that!"

In line with the three cars and against the barricade was a semi-truck, but with a few modifications. James quickly walked up, checking it out. The front end of the semi had two large pieces of thick metal attached that looked like a giant plow. There was a metal guard over the windshield and extra plating on the sides. It looked like a fortress. A zombie crawled out from under the semi and James jumped back, quickly drawing his tomahawk. In a swift move, he drove the spike into its brain and pulled it out. Another zombie was walking around the end of the barricade and Connor calmly walked over to it with his tomahawk out.

"This is what cleared the path," James said as Connor rejoined him, wiping blood off his tomahawk before sheathing it.

"That'd be my guess."

"I wonder if this was the caravan Tank was with."

"I don't see his truck."

"Me neither. They probably just went around."

James walked over to the right end of the barricade to make sure it was clear enough to get through. The ground was relatively flat and would be easy for the trucks to drive over. They'd have to watch the buses so they didn't get high-centered on the shoulder of the road, but they should be able to pass on this side.

He'd been about to turn around when something caught his eye. Walking over, he bent

down to examine it. A spike strip like law enforce-
ment officers used was hidden in the grass, and he
wondered what it was doing there. He looked
around, noticing there were a couple more hidden in
the grass between the interstate and the side of the
hill. Anyone trying to go around the right side of the
interstate would be screwed.

"Bro, you might want to come look at this,"
Connor said from over by one of the three vehicles
they'd guessed were part of a caravan.

James walked over, already dreading what
he knew they'd find. The entire right side and front
of the Toyota 4Runner was peppered with bullet
holes. Glancing back at the other two vehicles in the
caravan, they saw the same, including the minivan.
They hadn't noticed it before since they'd
approached on the left side of the vehicles, but now
it was blatantly obvious.

"It was an ambush," James said, looking at
his brother.

# 10
## AMBUSH

"We need to get back, now!" James said.

They moved into action, turning around and heading for the buses. James stopped short when he noticed someone standing on the hilltop to the west of where the buses were parked. The man raised an RPG over his shoulder. James took a knee and aimed through his scope, finding the man. In a hurry to get the man down, he fired, but his shot went wide. His brother fired behind him at the same time as the man fired and James watched in horror as the rocket flew into the side of the second bus. The bus exploded, flames reaching into the sky as screams split the air.

James watched as Emmett stepped on the gas and James's truck lurched forward. The remaining bus followed Emmett, and Alexis pulled around the flaming bus in her dad's truck. The man on the hill was down from Connor's shot, but more were now on top, firing at the vehicles below with assault rifles. He wanted to run to those in the flaming bus, but one look at it told him it wouldn't do any good.

James took his time finding his target on the hilltop and fired. The 5.56 bullet flew through the air two hundred and fifty-six yards to punch clean through the man's chest, exiting out his back in a spray of blood. Another man dropped from Connor's shot. Half of the group on the hilltop shifted their aim from the vehicles to the brothers kneeling next to the minivan. Bullets rained down around them as James and Connor dove behind cover. Emmett raced toward them. It looked like he was going to go around the barricade on the right side. Pulling the radio out of his vest, James quickly turned it on.

"Don't go to the right!" he yelled into the radio. "Go around on the left!"

"What about you?" Emmett asked.

James could hear glass shattering through the radio. He watched as Emmett raced toward them. *They're getting shot up!* Looking at his brother, he knew Connor was thinking along the same lines.

"Get the hell out of here!" James yelled into the radio.

There was a pause. "Roger that. Meet at the rendezvous."

James watched as Emmett veered to the left and the bus followed, along with the black Ford.

"Let's give them some cover fire!" Connor yelled.

James peeked around the back of the minivan and fired, taking down another shooter. He found his next target as he noticed a man aiming at them. The man dropped and James moved on. A bullet slammed into the minivan next to his face. He ducked behind cover as Emmett went around the left side of the barricade, followed by the bus. The bus went over the shoulder and looked like it might tip, but Greg was able to right it and they drove on. James stuck his head back behind cover and looked at his brother.

"We need to make a run for the other side of the barricade before they're fully focused on us," James said.

"I'll cover you," Connor said.

Connor leaned on the minivan's hood and fired rapidly as James took off. He ran straight for the next vehicle in line and stopped, turning around to fire wildly at the group as Connor ran to him. Connor paused for a second and then took off to the next rig while James covered him. Connor made it. James dropped out his empty magazine, replacing it with a full one. Connor began to fire and James ran to the next vehicle and past him to the decked-out semi. He opened fire and Connor ran to him.

"Let's go around the side of the barricade," James yelled as bullets slammed into the semi, the ground, and the other vehicles around them.

"They have a lot of fire focused on us!" Connor yelled.

"If we get stuck here, we're screwed!"

"You lead!"

*Lord, protect us!*

James ran from behind the semi as Connor began to fire at the hilltop. He ran around the back of a compact car, bullets hitting all around him. Diving over the car, he landed hard on the ground but instantly got up and moved to the next vehicle behind the barricade that offered more cover. He leaned over the hood and found one of the men in his scope and shot him. Picking another one off, he began to fire quicker as the men noticed him and fired on his position. Connor landed next to him with a curse and crawled over to him. James watched as Emmett's black truck turned the corner on the interstate and they were gone.

"Now what?" Connor asked, a hail of bullets descending all around them.

"Let's spread out," James said "Shoot once or twice, then move. They'll have a hard time pinning us down if we're on the move and staying low. Let's use their damn barricade against them."

Connor crawled farther along the line of vehicles, two or three wide in places, and James moved back to the car he first dove over. Lying on his belly, he crawled partway underneath the rear end so he could barely see the hill. There were nine men still on top. Five had left and another ten lay dead. His first shot took one of the men with a high-powered rifle in the chest. The other men looked for him but didn't see him at first as he lay hidden under the car. He fired again, taking down another. Then he crawled back behind cover and moved to another spot along the barricade.

James watched Connor shoot twice through the shattered window of a truck. James moved to another spot and leaned between a gap in two vehicles. The five remaining men on top lay prone and were a lot harder to hit now. He aimed at one and fired, hitting the man. A bullet whizzed through the air next to his head as his ear exploded with pain. He fell back behind cover, cursing. Bringing his hand up to his left ear, he felt that most of it was still intact, but a small chunk had been taken off the top.

*That was close,* James thought.

His brother cursed and dove to the ground.

"You hit?" James asked, crawling over to him.

"Yeah, but not bad," Connor said, looking at his right shoulder. James saw where a bullet had grazed him, cutting a groove in his flesh.

"You'll be fine," James said.

"I couldn't even get a shot off. Are you okay?"

"Oh, yeah. Just missing a piece of my ear." He could feel the blood running down the side of his face and neck.

"You'll be fine," Connor said with a smile.

James chuckled. "Touché. We need to come up with a plan. There's only four left."

"We need to do some *Enemy at the Gates* shooting."

"You know, that's not a bad idea," James said, looking at an RV.

It was parked on the other side of the barricade, but if they crawled under a truck they could get to the driver's door. It looked like all the curtains were down, and once inside they should be able to take out the rest.

"The RV," James said.

Connor looked at it. "Good plan."

James led the way, crawling under the truck. He peeked out from the other side and couldn't see the hilltop. It was hidden behind the RV. He stayed low and made his way to the driver's door, slowly opening it. A zombie pushed the door the rest of the way open and fell onto him. He was completely taken off guard as he fell onto his back, the zombie's mouth reaching for his neck. The spike of his brother's tomahawk took it in the side of the head and Connor rolled it off of him.

"Thanks, bro," James said as Connor helped him to a kneeling position.

"Pay attention," Connor growled.

"I know," James said. He moved back to the open door of the RV and looked inside. There were blankets over the passenger window and windshield, and all the curtains were down.

*Perfect,* James thought, slowly getting inside.

Moving further in, he had his tomahawk ready just in case. The RV was empty and he moved to the back room, noticing glass all over the floor. The windows had been shattered. Just what he wanted. He looked to see Connor climbing into the loft above the windshield and lay down with a small window in front of him. James crawled behind the bed in the back and watched as a light breeze blew the curtains. He got a good look at the hilltop when the curtains moved. Grabbing the pillows, he rested his AR on the bed and covered it with them, except the end of the scope and barrel.

The curtains fluttered and he found the hilltop, but they moved back into place before he could get a shot. He didn't move. Aiming at the spot where he'd seen the hilltop, he waited. The curtains fluttered again and his view cleared. He found one of the men and fired. James couldn't tell if he'd hit the man he was aiming at or not. His brother fired twice right after him. The wind blew the curtains back open. The man James had shot at before was still lying there, very much alive.

*Damn, I missed,* he thought as he shot him in the head—not missing this time. The last man stood up and began to run to the other side of the hill. Connor shot and the man dropped to the ground as the curtain moved back in front of the window.

Cautiously, James went to the window and gently pulled aside the curtain to get a look. All the men on the hilltop were dead, and if he'd counted right, they'd gotten them all. He watched the hilltop for another minute until he was satisfied.

"I think we got 'em," James said, moving over to his brother, who was climbing out of the loft.

"I think you're right," Connor said. "Let's get one of these vehicles running and catch up with Emmett."

"Sounds like a plan," James said, getting out of the RV.

Smoke rose in the distance from the fire that still consumed the entire school bus that'd been full of people just minutes before. Now, it was a burning husk of death. He knew no one would've been able to survive that. He was relieved that Olive was in his truck or she could've been on that bus. Not that his truck was much safer. She still could've been hit with a bullet and died in the backseat, but he pushed the thought from his mind. Until he knew for sure, he wouldn't dwell on it. It wouldn't do any good. There would've been at least thirty people on that bus. Even though it wasn't directly his fault, he still felt responsible for all their deaths. He'd missed the shot and they'd paid the price.

"Brother, it's not your fault," Connor said, getting out behind him and resting a hand on his shoulder. "They would've all been dead if we hadn't rescued them from the school. That horde would've eventually gotten inside the gym and it would've been a mass slaughter. Even the ones who've died were able to enjoy life that much longer."

"I know, but I wanted to save them, not just prolong their lives."

"You don't have that kind of power. You can do your best to help and protect them, but in the end it's not contingent on anything you do. It's out of your hands, James."

James took a deep breath and let it out. "You're right." Even though he said it and knew it to be true, he'd carry the weight of their deaths to his grave.

"Good, now we need to worry about getting out of here so we can join up with Emmett."

"Let's find a ride."

Bullet holes decorated most of the vehicles, and their options didn't look good. James moved to the west side of the barricade and looked at a promising Subaru. Checking it for dead things, he climbed inside and looked around for the keys. Not finding any, he looked under the dash for wires he could cut and touch together to start it. He quickly discovered that despite how easy the movies made it look, he had no idea how to hot-wire a car. Climbing out, he looked off to the side of the road where two vehicles were crashed into each other. He stopped dead in his tracks, not believing what he saw.

"Connor, you need to see this!"

Connor came running over, AR ready, and looked where James was pointing.

"I'll be damned," Connor said, looking at the maroon Avalanche crashed into the side of a Ranger.

They approached the two vehicles, cautious and dreading what they might find. Walking up, James noticed a zombie in the backseat of the Avalanche, arms stretched toward them. He pulled out his tomahawk and drove the spike into its eye. It sagged in the seat. Looking in the truck, he found no other bodies, much to his relief.

"I don't see him," James said.

Connor looked around, noticing something past the truck, and walked over to it while James checked the truck one more time. There was blood in the backseat but nothing in the front. He hadn't died there. Moving around, he opened the tailgate and removed the bed cover. There were a few bags, mostly filled with clothes, but one backpack had some food, water, and survival items. Connor walked back over as James climbed out of the truck bed.

"There was another one over there," Connor said, pointing to the west. "Shot in the back and paralyzed."

"He left in a hurry," James said, showing him the black backpack.

"That's definitely his," Connor said, taking it. "What do you think?"

"I think he tried to get away when the shooting started and that Ranger drove in front. Then they bailed out, heading west. Most of the fire was on the east side of the vehicles."

"And there's a gradual decline over there, perfect if you were trying to escape gunfire."

"So he went west."

"Then that's the way we go," Connor said, throwing the backpack over his shoulders.

"You didn't see anything useful at the barricade, did you? Like guns?"

"Nope, they cleaned it out."

"That's what I thought," James said, looking to the Bighorn Mountains in the distance.

He'd always loved this stretch of the road when he went to Fort Collins to visit Tank. Thinking back to those times, he shook his head. It felt like a lifetime ago, and it was unreal to think that it hadn't even been a full week yet. Not even a week into the apocalypse and they'd lost so much. It didn't bode well.

How were they going to survive or ever get to Alaska when they couldn't even go half a day without something tragic happening? Here they were again at the receiving end of their new life, which was going to hell in a hand basket. It left them with only two options—either they stood up, brushed themselves off and moved forward, or they sat down and died. It was an easy choice. They weren't about to do any sitting anytime soon.

"How much ammo you got?" James asked his brother, looking down at his own vest.

"Full handgun and four extra mags, but only three left for my AR. I went through almost four back there," Connor said.

"I did go through four, so I have a little under three."

"Time to use our melee weapons for the zombies."

"And no more firefights."

"We gonna do this?"

"Let's go find Tank," James said.

Side-by-side they walked toward the Bighorn Mountains while the sun sank lower in the sky before them.

# 11
# THE MOUNTAINS ARE CALLING

Cresting the hill, James looked down at US-87 as it lay below them. There was a house on the side of the highway at the bottom of the hill. Another house with trees around it sat opposite the road. It looked like a small creek paralleled the road on the west, with green fields surrounding it.

"Let's check the closest house," James said as they walked down the hill. His ear was throbbing, but he did his best to ignore it.

Approaching the house from the back, they swung their ARs to their sides. Connor drew his suppressed handgun while James took out his tomahawk. A sliding-glass door was open and a dead zombie was lying inside on the floor. Its head had been pulverized and a bloody rock lay beside it.

"Someone's been here," James said as they moved into the house.

The back door brought them into an open kitchen and dining room area with a door to their right and two to their left. All the doors were open. James moved to the right doorway. Inside was the master bedroom, with a door open to the bathroom. Both rooms were clear and no guns were hidden in the nightstand or closet. Moving back out to the dining room, he went through the door on the opposite wall. It was an office of sorts and empty of threats. Taking a second, he looked in all the obvious places for a weapon and only came up with a letter opener, which he left for someone who might actually need it. The other door led to a hallway with a set of stairs going down. Moving through the hall, James briefly glanced in an open doorway on the right, leading to an empty two-car garage with one of the large doors open.

"Down first," James said.

Connor nodded.

He moved to the top of the stairs and hesitated. The last time he'd been in a basement it had been horrifying. Conquering his fears, he tried to flip the lights on but they didn't work. He pulled the flashlight off the rails of his AR. With the flashlight in one hand and tactical tomahawk in the other, James moved down the stairs. Connor was a step behind with his flashlight and handgun. At the bottom of the stairs, James released a breath he didn't even know he'd been holding. The basement was open with an entertainment center in the right corner behind the stairs and two open doorways on the far wall. Carefully moving throughout the basement, the brothers found it to be devoid of zombies or anything useful. They moved back to the top of the stairs.

"We should probably clean our wounds," James said, returning to the kitchen.

Pulling out a large bowl, he turned the faucet on and was rewarded with a little bit of water. Connor walked to the master bedroom.

Getting a clean washcloth from a drawer, James wiped the blood off the side of his face and neck. He was careful not to irritate the wound and cause it to bleed again. When he finished cleaning, Connor came out with a small box of Band-Aids.

"This is all they've got," Connor said.

"Put it in the pack. Let's check the house across the street. Then if we have to, we'll use those."

Connor tossed them to him and turned around. James put them in the backpack and they moved to the garage. Walking in, James noticed something he hadn't before when he'd glanced in. A message was spray-painted on the wall: Anddersons, going to mountains, people chasing us. Meet you. Tank.

"No freakin' way. He *is* alive," Connor said.

"Holy crap!" James said, grinning. "Well, he didn't make it very far after he called us. That means they probably would've come through here last night. Let's go check that house across the street and hopefully find a car. Then we have to decide on what to do—go after Tank or meet up with our group."

"Damn…"

"Yeah, let's go."

Exiting the garage, they walked down to the road, turning south. James led the way, his mind a jumble of thoughts. As far as they knew, Tank was still alive, but he'd gone into the mountains, chased by the same people who'd set up the ambush. He'd need help, but how would they find him? There might only be a handful of roads leading into the mountains, but they could easily miss each other and be looking for weeks. Emmett and the girls would be waiting for them. They couldn't just ditch them, especially little Olive. They could meet Emmett and then head after Tank, but what about the rest of the group? Would they leave them or drag them along? There was no easy decision and he dreaded having to make it. He knew which way he was leaning but didn't want to even admit it to himself. Things were getting more and more complicated by the hour.

After walking a few hundred yards they arrived at the turnoff for the next house. Trees lined the road and both sides of the dirt driveway, obscuring their view of anything on the property.

"There was a house here, right?" Connor asked.

"Yeah, it's tucked behind the trees," James said. He remembered seeing it from the top of the hill.

"That's what I thought. Keep your head on a swivel."

James nodded and they started down the driveway. Once the trees opened up, they noticed there were over six buildings spread out on the property—two large pole barns, a shed, two stables, a detached garage and a house. He moved to the house first. They'd clear it and then check the garage and barns for a vehicle. Posting up at the front door, Connor opened it and James went into the house. The kitchen was in front of him, along with the dining room, and a door led off to the left. James moved to the door and Connor opened it. Going into the room, James noticed a set of stairs directly to his left with a door in front of him halfway into the room.

Something inside was groaning and weakly scratching at the door. Connor moved to the door as James stopped a few steps back from it and nodded. Connor opened the door. A zombie stumbled out, arms reaching for him. Its face was met with the spike of a tomahawk and it fell to the ground before he could pull the weapon free. Instead of going for the weapon, he immediately drew his handgun and aimed at a second zombie coming through the doorway. Firing, the suppressed 1911 made a muffled crack as the zombie fell to the ground, a .45 caliber bullet hole in its head. Nothing else came out of the room. James holstered his handgun and reached for his tomahawk that was embedded in the first zombie's skull.

"We good?" Connor whispered, aiming into the room.

"Yeah, let's clear it."

Going through the doorway, James tried to ignore the blood-splattered bed. His mind flashed back to a different master bedroom covered in blood, with small bodies scattered on the floor. Shaking the memory from his head, he moved to the other door. Inside was a bathroom with a first aid kit under the sink.

"Score!" James said, pulling it out. "Let me see your shoulder."

Connor closed the bathroom door and pulled up his sleeve, exposing the shallow graze in his shoulder. It looked like it hurt, but he knew the alternative was worse. If the bullet had been a few inches to the left, it would've been devastating, if not deadly. Using one of the antiseptic wipes, James cleaned the wound and then put antibiotic ointment on it. Finally, he wrapped gauze around his brother's shoulder. James could only remember part of his wilderness first aid training, but he remembered that cleaning the wound was first and foremost, and he'd done that. They would check it in a day or two and make sure it wasn't infected. The graze was shallow enough that they shouldn't have to worry about it though.

"Your turn," Connor said, pulling his sleeve down.

"Yay," James said without enthusiasm.

Connor cleaned James's wound, then leaned back, examining it.

"I have no idea what to do here. You're missing a chunk of your ear and I can't figure out how to help. Should I wrap a bandage clear around your head? Or just your ear? Or just stick a Band-Aid on it and call it good?"

"Well... hell, I don't know." James looked in the mirror, assessing his ear. He could see that the missing chunk was probably the size of a dime taken off the top of his left ear. The more he looked at it, the more he realized it hurt. But he couldn't for the life of him think of a way to bandage it properly. "I guess just soak some gauze and wrap my ear. Then put one wrap around my head to hold it in place."

"That'll have to do," Connor said as he went to work. In a few minutes he had a redneck-looking bandage on James's ear. "It doesn't look pretty, but it should hold."

"Feels better, I think. But I already feel an itch coming on."

"Sucks to be you."

"Yeah," James said, chuckling as he packed up the rest of the first aid kit and shoved it into the backpack. "Let's check upstairs and then go get a ride."

"You decide what we're doing yet?" Connor whispered as they left the bathroom.

"I'm trying *not* to think about it, actually."

"Well, you'd better decide because you know where I stand. Tank is blood."

"I know." But that didn't make this decision any easier; in fact, it made it a whole lot harder.

Climbing the stairs, James took the lead. At the top, the room opened up to an entertainment center with a door to the left. Hearing a thump on the other side of the door, James moved to it and waited for Connor. Once in position, James nodded. Connor opened the door. It was no zombie but a man armed with a Colt 1911 handgun. James lunged forward but knew he wouldn't make it in time. The man had the safety off and the gun leveled at James's forehead. James didn't see his life flash before his eyes—he didn't think at all—he just tried to act quickly. Being so focused on the gun and the threat of dying, he didn't look at the man until he had his tomahawk cocked behind his head, about to bring it down on the man's hands.

"Tank?" James asked, standing frozen, his tomahawk raised over his shoulder. He'd just about attacked his best friend!

"James? What the bloody hell are you doin' here?" Tank asked, lowering his handgun.

"What?" Connor said, coming from behind the door. "It *is* you!"

"Holy…!" James said, sheathing the tomahawk and giving Tank a huge hug.

"I didn't think I'd see you guys here," Tank said as he released James.

Connor and Tank embraced, patting each other on the back.

"We didn't think you were here either. We were about to head into the mountains after you!"

"Oh yeah," Tank said, chuckling. "That was for the asshats following us."

"Us?" James asked.

"James, Connor, meet Chloe."

A woman in her twenties stepped into the doorway and gave a little wave.

"And this is Selena."

From the other side of the doorway, an older woman with dark hair and a square face emerged.

"Nice to meet you. I'm James."

"Connor," his brother said.

"Hi," Chloe said.

"Nice to meet you two," Selena said.

"Wait, so you left the note and have been hiding out here ever since?" James asked.

"Sorta. We vandalized the wall, stole a 'stang, took it for a joyride, looped around and parked it in the barn, then hung out in here all day. We were going to head north tomorrow, but I wanted to make sure those bastards weren't following us still."

"Yeah, we know those guys. They hit our group too. We lost at least thirty," James said.

"Ah hell, I'm sorry guys. Those pricks deserve a reckoning."

"We got a few of 'em," Connor said.

"Good. Serves 'em right," Tank said.

"So what've you been doing all day?" James asked, looking around the messy room and disheveled bed.

"Oh, you know. We found somethin' to do," Tank said with a wink.

"Oh shut the hell up you perv," Chloe said. "I'd never even touch you."

"See what I get for saving her ass?" Tank said.

"We've been playing board games," Selena said, shaking her head as she pointed to the Monopoly and Risk boxes laying on the floor.

James and Connor burst out laughing.

"I almost believed you," James said, cracking up.

"I had to try," Tank said, smiling.

"What, you forgot Munchkins?" Connor joked.

"The game's in my pack," Tank said. "And my pack's in my truck."

"That's a shame," James said as Connor turned to the side so Tank could get a view of the backpack.

"Hell yeah! You guys rock," Tank said. "It's good to be back together!"

"Hell yeah, it is," Connor said.

"Well, let's get out of here," James said. "We have some people to meet."

Smiling, the three friends led the women from the bedroom. James couldn't believe Tank was alive and here of all places. He'd been hoping he'd be okay, but he hadn't dared hope for more. Now that they were together, they'd be able to take on anything they faced. They'd meet Emmett and the girls and continue their trek to Alaska, together. Everything was finally starting to look up.

"So where's Frostmourne?" James asked as they walked downstairs.

"Lost it in FoCo, plus the damn thing was so heavy. Completely impractical. I should've grabbed one of the other dozen weapons I had hanging on my wall. But I mean, come on, it's not every day you can go around slaying undead yelling, 'Hail to the king, baby.'"

"That's true," James said, chuckling. Tank led the way from the house and continued toward the barn a few hundred yards away.

"Shotgun," Connor called when they were halfway across the yard.

"Dammit," James said.

"You've always been a little slow on that Jamesy Boy," Tank said.

"Come on, not that nickname or I'll tell everyone your real name."

"I already told the girls my name. Being stuck in a room all day with two talkative girls will make a man do some dangerous things. But they promised not to use it, right girls?"

"Don't count on it, *Arthas Menethil*," Chloe said, putting emphasis on the name with a sweet smile.

The brothers burst out laughing so hard they couldn't continue walking as they doubled over in mirth.

"What?" Chloe said.

"Sweetie, I told you that wasn't his real name," Selena said.

"But he was so reluctant and honest!" Chloe exclaimed. "He even teared up when he said he hadn't told anyone since this all started!"

Tank chuckled, a mischievous glint in his eye. "Sorry, baby, I had to."

"You dick," Chloe said angrily, which made the brothers laugh even harder.

After a few minutes, they stood up straight. Their raucous laughter quieted down to a chuckle.

"You, my friend, are a genius," James said. "Now, no more jokes or we'll draw all the zombies within five miles."

"I can't make any promises," Tank said as they continued to the barn where a black Ford Mustang sat. The car had red racing stripes the length of the body and looked brand new.

"Nice ride," Connor said.

"Thanks, just bought it," Tank said. "Only like a hundred miles on it."

"We need to customize the rear window," James said, looking at it. The Mustang was a two-door sports car, and if they got into a gunfight the people in the backseat wouldn't be able to shoot. "Just in case we get in a pinch."

"But, my baby…" Tank said, deflated.

"Sorry, buddy."

Pulling out of the driveway, Tank hit the gas and they sped off on US-87, the sun setting behind the mountains to their left. It was great to have the Wolf Pack back together. It'd been years since the three of them had been able to hang out at the same time. With Tank living in Colorado, James in Montana, and Connor in the corps, it'd been hard to coordinate. But now here they were, together at the end of the world. What were the chances?

*It's not just by chance,* said a voice in James's head.

The voice was right. It hadn't been just by chance they'd survived and found each other in a random house.

James said a quick prayer: *Thanks God, if you could keep helping and guiding us, that'd be awesome!*

In the front seat, Connor had a small smile on his face and so did Tank.

*Yes, it's good to be back together,* James thought, smiling also.

"So what the hell are we doing?" Tank asked.

"We're meeting Emmett and the rest of our group somewhere on this road. I already told you about Alexis and Ana, but we picked up a lot more in Burns, Wyoming," James said. "We started out with over a hundred and are now down to thirty-some."

"Wow, that's harsh," Tank said. "I won't ask how."

James nodded as they sped down the highway. The wind from the missing back window whipped the girls' hair around. "We can talk about that later," he said.

"Sounds good, but did you have to get glass everywhere?" Tank asked, pulling a piece from underneath him and throwing it out the window.

"Sorry, but now I can shoot," James said. "Plus, if we're getting shot at, chances are it'll break anyway."

"You're right," Tank said, "But next time lets plan something a little better than just smashing it."

"Granted, it wasn't my best idea," James said, smiling.

"Definitely not," Connor said.

"This sucks," Chloe said, her brunette hair whipping wildly in the wind.

"I don't mind it. Feels good," Selena said, her short black hair not as affected.

"Anyone have a hair tie?" Chloe asked.

"Oh yeah, I always keep one on hand," Tank said, and for a moment it seemed like she believed him. Then her face soured.

"I have one, sweetie," Selena said, taking one out of her pocket.

"Thanks."

"Fine then," Tank said, putting a hair tie into his pocket.

Chloe ignored Tank and Connor looked over at him curiously.

"I just found it in the cup holder," Tank whispered to him.

Connor chuckled. "You're a piece."

Tank smiled. "So James, what happened to your ear?"

"Those bastards at the ambush shot a chunk of it off," James said, gently touching it.

Tank laughed. "That blows."

"Yeah, tell me about it," James said.

"So we just continue on this until… what?" Tank asked.

"Emmett said he'd meet us on US-87 somewhere, so I guess we take this until we meet him or hit I-90," James said.

"Do you know where it hits I-90?" Tanks asked.

James shrugged.

"In Sheridan," Selena said.

"Well, hell," Tank said. "So much for avoiding big cities."

# 12
# TO BUILD A FIRE

Houses were becoming more frequent as US-87 merged with another highway, turning to the northeast. Zombies became more numerous as well. Tank had to actively work at avoiding them.

*It's not as easy when you don't have a truck to run them over with,* James thought.

If they weren't careful they could high-center or wreck the car by hitting one. Tank was a good driver, however, and he weaved around them as they continued to grow more prolific.

"Damn, they're everywhere," Tank said as they drove past a group of four zombies that tried to follow them, staggering behind the car like drunks chasing a butterfly.

"We need to get on I-90 as soon as we can and get north of town. Hopefully, Emmett did the same," James said.

"What about the radio?" Connor asked. "Might work now that we're closer."

"I'll try," James said as he pulled it out. "Emmett, do you copy?"

Static played over the radio and he tried again without success.

"Worth a try," Connor said as James put the radio back.

"It means he's more than likely north of Sheridan, hopefully. I'll try again when we get closer," James said.

"How far will one of those reach?" Selena asked.

"Maybe a few miles," James said.

"In perfect conditions," Connor said.

"So about as far as you can throw 'em," Tank said.

"Ah," Selena said.

"Is that a person?" Chloe asked, pointing ahead.

"What?" James asked, looking forward. She must have seen a zombie or something. Surely no one would be walking around out here alone.

"She's right," Connor said. "He just ran off the right side of the road."

James stood up through the broken window and aimed at the spot with his AR. Connor stuck his out the window. As they drew near, Tank slowed the Mustang to a stop. James could see something poking out from behind a tree ten yards off the road.

"I see you there," James said. "Come out and we won't shoot."

A tall, lanky boy stepped out, hands in the air. He appeared to be in his mid-teens and had light brown hair. He wore an orange backpack and a ragged green jacket with an old single-action revolver tucked into the front of his pants.

"Well, at least you're not the Reclaimers," the teen said, smiling.

"Who?" James asked, keeping the teen in his scope.

"The crazy people around here who like to shoot first and ask questions later," the teen said.

"What's your name?" James asked.

"Mike," he said.

"So, Mike, what are you doing out here alone? You are alone, right?"

"Of course I am. And, you know, just playing hide and seek with the zombs."

"You don't have a group?"

"I did, but the Reclaimers killed them all and took me prisoner."

"You escaped?"

"Isn't that obvious?"

"Show some respect to the man who holds your life in his hands, boy," Tank said.

"What? Like I'm scared of you? I could die at any second by the zombs or Reclaimers. So what if you're the one to do it?"

"Just calm down," James said. "So you escaped and now here you are?"

"Pretty much. Been running for a couple days, trying to get out, but they have the interstate and a lot of the roads blocked."

"Yeah, we know," Tank said.

"Have you seen anyone else on the road?" James asked.

"You mean like other people? No. But zombs? Plenty."

"We're looking for the rest of our group."

"Where'd you see 'em last?" Mike asked.

"I-90 at the barricade. They broke through and went north. We're hoping to meet up with them."

"You'll never see them again," Mike said with a chuckle.

"Do you need an ass kickin'?" Tank asked.

"Why do you say that?" James asked Mike. He agreed with Tank. This punk needed to be decked right in his smug face.

"Reclaimers have another spot they catch people at. The good news is, if you make it past their first 'trial' they let you live and just take you prisoner."

"Sounds like they're crazy," Connor said.

"Oh yeah, or at least their leader is, straight up mental. The rest just want any excuse to shoot people or zombs, doesn't matter which."

"Great," Tank said. "More insane bastards. Not like there wasn't already enough in FoCo."

"Yeah, so can I hop in with you?" Mike asked. "I'll give you all my weapons. I just want to get out of here."

"Tank? Connor?" James asked.

"Sure, the more the merrier," Tank said. "Plus, if he pisses me off, I'll just punch him in the nose."

"I'll take your weapons," Connor said.

"Rad," Mike said, walking over and pulling out his pistol and a knife from his boot, giving them both to Connor. "Where am I gonna sit?"

"Just like me," James said as he scooted all the way over, sitting above the backseat with his feet on the seat.

"This majorly sucks," Chloe said as she scrunched next to James's legs.

"Hello, ladies, I'm Mike," he said as he climbed up on the trunk and sat down like James.

"Yeah, we heard," Selena said. "If you step on me, I'll throw you off the back."

"Man, you're all so hostile."

"Comes with the times," Tank said as he pressed on the gas and the car lurched forward.

Mike's arms flailed in the air and he almost flipped off the back but gathered his balance at the last second. "Hey!"

Tank and Connor laughed and James barely held his mirth in check.

"Tank," James said.

"Just making sure everyone knows to hold on tight."

"I'm as good as dead," Mike said, gripping tightly to the roof and doorjamb in front of him.

"Yep," Tank said as he topped out at a good cruising speed and they continued north.

A few minutes later, they were in the southern part of Sheridan. Tank drove to the nearest intersection and turned right, heading toward the interstate. Abandoned and crashed vehicles were scattered everywhere, complete with zombies. James was amazed. It looked like a lot of this destruction was fresh—maybe only a couple of days old. The zombies began to stumble toward them.

"This place hasn't been like this long," James said.

"No, that's why we were heading this way," Mike said. "It was supposed to be in good shape."

"So much for that," Connor said.

"Yeah, it's gone now," Tank said, turning onto the off ramp for the interstate.

"What're you doing?" Chloe asked.

"Are you serious?" Tank asked. "It's the end of the world. There're no vehicles driving around and you want me to pass that huge horde of undead to get on the interstate the right way?"

"Well... never mind," Chloe said, clearly flustered.

"I can see why you'd initially think that," James said, trying to alleviate some of the tension. "It's an honest mistake."

"Don't patronize me," Chloe snapped.

"Okay..." James said, turning back to the task at hand—keeping a lookout for Emmett or anything else they might come across. This woman was seriously frustrating. He was beginning to see why Tank treated her the way he did. Then again, Tank treated everyone like that at some point or another.

"I wouldn't try," Tank said. "The more you try to help, the pissier she gets."

"Only with *you*," Chloe said.

"No question there," Tank said.

"I guess it's not just me you hate then," Mike said.

"No, I pretty much hate everyone," Tank said. "The undead were supposed to take care of that, but they failed on a few, I see."

"If I didn't know better, I'd say you started all this," Mike said, eyeing Tank.

"Of course I did! I'm Arthas Menethil!" Tank said with a laugh.

"Nice reference," Mike said.

"You know what he's talking about?" Selena asked.

"Of course. Arthas is the Lich King in *World of Warcraft*. He controls the Scourge, a faction of the undead," Mike said enthusiastically.

"Maybe you're not all bad," Tank said.

"What are you talking about?" Chloe asked.

"It's a video game," James said.

"Figures," Chloe said. "I'm stuck in a vehicle with a bunch of children at the end of the world."

"When you say it like that, it does sound kind of depressing," Mike said. "How about, 'The end of the world has come and my companions are masters of the lore of Azeroth.'"

"Much better," James said.

"I like that," Tank said.

"You're all a bunch of nerds!" Chloe said, exasperated.

"Thanks," Mike and Tank said at the same time.

"Jinx!" Mike said.

"Dude, no one does that anymore," Tank said.

"You still owe me a soda."

"Fine," Tank said, then whispered to Connor. "But I'm going to shake it up first."

"I heard that," Mike said.

"Damn, guess I'll have to try that on the next one who jinxes me."

"I thought you said no one does—"

The vehicle swerved hard to the right. Mike tumbled off the back, crashing to the pavement. Even with swerving, Tank hadn't been able to avoid it. He'd seen it too late. The spike strip tore through the driver's side tires. It took all that Tank had to keep them from flipping. Their momentum caused them to crash into the side of an SUV, but they'd slowed down enough that the airbags didn't even deploy. James ended up on top of the girls in the backseat. He picked himself up and climbed out the back window. Already, zombies were beginning to stumble toward them and Mike, who was kneeling with a hand to his head.

"You got them?" James asked, looking at Connor.

"Go," Connor said, climbing out of the Mustang.

James took off running to Mike, his ear beginning to throb from the exertion. Crouching down next to him, he raised his AR and shot the two closest zombies, dropping them to the pavement.

"You okay?" James asked as Mike removed his hand. James looked at it, aside from some road rash, he looked fine. "Did you hit your head?"

"Not when I landed. I fell on my ass. I may have broken my tailbone," Mike said.

"Okay, let's get you up and see if you can walk," James said, helping him stand. "Good thing we weren't going much faster or this could have been a lot worse."

"No crap. What happened?"

"Spike strip."

James hauled Mike to his feet, and after a few limping steps, he was able to walk on his own.

"My hip freaking hurts too."

"You're good for now. The more you walk, the better you'll feel."

They made it back to the group, who were all out of the car, standing next to it.

Connor shot the nearest zombie, then looked back at them. "We need to go."

James looked around, realizing there were more zombies than he thought scattered around the vehicles on the interstate.

"I'd say," Tank said.

"Is that a used car lot over there?" Selena asked, pointing into town to the west of the interstate.

"I think so. Let's go," James said.

"Here," Connor said, giving Mike his revolver and knife back. "Don't use your handgun unless you have to."

"Thanks. I'll let you two do all the shooting. I only have three bullets left anyway."

Hopping over the guardrail, James led the way down the small embankment into the northern end of Sheridan. Tank followed behind him with the girls next, then Mike, and finally Connor bringing up the rear. Crossing the train tracks, they entered town and stopped at the back of a department store.

"Here," Connor said, offering Tank his tomahawk.

"Entering stealth mode," Tank said.

"Really? You're joking in a situation like this?" Chloe asked.

"Of course. These are the best times for joking."

"You hang here. I'm gonna go check it out," James said. "But I don't think that's a used car lot."

"No, it looks like a junkyard," Connor said.

James ran in a crouch from behind the department store. Luckily, as big cities go, Sheridan wasn't that big. There were still too many zombies for his liking though. Running across the street, two zombies took notice of him. He drew his tomahawk and took care of the first one, then moved on to the second, ending it with a spike to its skull. Moving to the fence that surrounded the yard, he found a shorter section and climbed over. As he dropped to the ground a couple of feet below, he realized that was exactly what this was—a junkyard.

While some of the vehicles looked usable, he decided they'd have better luck elsewhere. He approached an old school bus that was missing its tires, planning to climb it to get a better look at the surrounding area, but stopped suddenly. He could see the children's faces behind the windows, being burned alive as flames consumed them. Their screams tore through the silence of the evening and he watched in horror as he could do nothing to save them.

James shook his head, breathing heavily and realized he was sweating. He looked again at the school bus sitting there. It wasn't the one full of kids but an old rusty one in the middle of the junkyard.

*What the hell was that?* he thought.

He looked down at his tomahawk shaking in his hand. Taking a deep breath, he tried his best to clear his mind, but that image was still burned into his subconscious. Shaking his head again, he growled and climbed up onto the hood of the school bus. His ear began throbbing and the pain returned. Even though it wasn't vital, his missing piece of ear was sure a pain in the ass. He wondered if cutting the whole damn thing off would help. He knew it wouldn't—this was just turning out to be an annoying wound.

On the roof of the bus James shivered, the sweat on his skin turning cold. The wind was picking up, and even on this warm summer evening, it brought an unexpected chill from the mountains. Immediately, he spotted a used car dealership across the main drag. It looked like there were quite a few vehicles in good shape. The only problem was that there were zombies scattered all around town, especially between them and the dealership. They'd need to think of something to lure them away because there was no way they were getting past them.

Connor watched as his brother jumped off the bus, climbed over the fence and ran back, taking down another zombie along the way.

"Okay," James said. "That's definitely a junkyard, but there's a used car dealership across the road."

"Sweet," Tank said. "Anything big and mean-lookin'?"

"Couldn't tell. There are a lot of vehicles though. But we have a problem."

"Wouldn't expect anything less," Tank said.

"There are too many zombies between us and it. We need to draw 'em off."

"Of course," Mike said, sighing.

"What's the plan?" Connor asked.

"There's a gas station a little farther to the north—"

"Finally, I get to blow some shit up!" Tank said.

"Exactly," James said. "We'll blow it up and the explosion and fire should draw 'em."

"Aren't you worried about the fire spreading?" Chloe asked.

"And what? Takin' more undead out with it?" Tank said.

"It doesn't look like there're any houses nearby, just a bunch of businesses," James said, "And the wind blowing this hard will keep the fire from catching the trees to the west."

"So, how do we blow it?" Tank asked, that mischievous glint returning to his eyes.

"Not sure," James answered.

"A flaming arrow!" Mike said.

"Do you have a bow? Or even an arrow, for that matter?" Tank asked.

"Well, no."

"Do you expect us to have one hidden somewhere?"

"Okay, okay. It was a bad idea. What if you just shoot a pump?"

"Won't work. Haven't you ever seen *Myth Busters*?" James asked.

"Yeah, just not that episode," Mike said, crestfallen.

"Let's head over there and see if we can't think of something," James said. "I have a few ideas. It's just that they're all dangerous."

"So, the best kind of ideas," Tank said.

James led the way, with Connor bringing up the rear. Connor had never blown up a gas station before, but it was on his bucket list. He wondered if normal people had blowing stuff up on their bucket lists. Most people probably didn't, but all the cool ones did, and he knew for a fact that a lot of his Marine buddies wanted to. So maybe it was a military thing. Well, that and arsonists, but they took it a little too far.

Watching Mike in front of him, Connor found himself beginning to like the kid. While he was mouthy and kind of a dunce, he had a good heart. The realization made him angry. There wasn't a place in this new world for attachments. He had his Wolf Pack with him, but other than those two, he didn't need anyone. Everyone else would either let him down or die, just like the little dark-haired kid in the apartment. He felt a swelling of emotion but wrestled it back down. Those feelings could get him killed in a situation like this—they had no place here.

Following the back side of the department store, they went around it to the north. There weren't any buildings on that side, just the interstate and therefore not as many zombies. The few they did encounter, James and Tank took care of with the tomahawks. Connor felt naked without his, but then he remembered he was holding a badass instrument of death.

Moving through the parking lot, they arrived at the main road going south into town. James ran across the road to the other side where a small white building sat on the edge of a large vacant lot. The rest of the group followed. Connor watched them all run across, covering them. When it was his turn, he followed. Crouching behind the white building, they all looked at the gas station.

"Looks like it's our lucky day," Tank said.

A few zombies were wandering around, but most of them were concentrated farther into town. Sitting next to one of the pumps was a semi-truck with a cylinder-shaped trailer.

"That'll work," Connor said, looking at the fuel truck.

"But how, exactly?" James asked.

"Crash a car into it?" Mike offered.

"Not a bad idea. Tank, you're good at that," James said.

"Really? There was a spike strip!" Tank said defensively.

"I'm talking about your Avalanche back there. What does that make? Three trucks you've wrecked?"

"Oh, you're an ass!" Tank said. "You know I only wrecked one before. The other one the damn lady rear-ended me! Plus, that last one doesn't count. The Ranger pulled in front of me."

"Sure," James said, smiling.

"James, I'm going to throttle you," Tank said only half-joking.

Connor chuckled. "It's still not a bad idea."

"No, it's not. It's just highly dangerous trying to jump out of a moving vehicle and hoping it continues on with enough force to cause the trailer to explode," James said.

"What about draining the gas from the trailer? It's close enough to the pumps that if it goes up, the whole thing will," Connor said.

"Molotov!" Mike said triumphantly.

James started to open his mouth but then looked at the gas station. "Kid, that's a damn good idea."

Connor burst through the doors of the gas station, AR sweeping left and right. Tank entered behind him, tomahawk at the ready. He was in a small entry room with a counter on his left, a room to the right that looked like it held showers, and the main room of the station in front. Cautiously moving further into the building, he entered the main room with its mostly raided shelves and wall coolers.

"Clear," Connor said. "Where do they keep the booze?"

"What? Just because I'm a bartender means I know where every gas station across the United Sates keeps their liquor?" Tank asked.

Connor looked at him and shrugged.

"Damn, you got me." Tank walked even further into the room and looked around. "Wyoming has liquor laws on wine and the hard stuff. A gas station like this won't carry any."

"Okay, let's think about this. If you had to work in a gas station all day, would you just sit behind the counter, sober?"

"Hell no. That job would suck."

"Let's hope someone else shared your opinion."

"You think someone has something stashed in here?"

"Maybe. Check behind the counter. I'll get the back room," Connor said, switching to his handgun.

He walked back to a small alcove with four doors, two to his left and two to his right. The first door on the right looked like a storage room with a couple of desks inside. Going in, he cleared the room, then walked over to the nicer of the two desks. Inside one of the drawers was not only a half-empty bottle of whiskey but a snub-nose Ruger .357 revolver in a shoulder holster. He swung the pack off his back and stuffed the revolver inside. Grabbing a rag from beside the desk, he left the storage room and turned back toward the main room.

A sound from behind made him turn. He noticed the door to the men's restroom swing open and a zombie stumbled out. It looked at him and groaned, trying to take a step forward, but tripped over the pants pulled down around its ankles. Its face cracked against the floor and Connor had to chuckle as he stomped his boot down hard on its head. Its already weakened skull cracked under the force and caved in, blood and brains splattering the floor.

"Talk about dying with your pants down," Tank said, walking over. "Nice curb stomp, by the way."

"Thanks. Not the most dignified way to go, that's for sure," Connor said, leaving the alcove. "I got what we need, plus a new toy."

"Sweet, then let's…" Tank said, pausing for dramatic effect, "… blow this joint!"

"You're terrible," Connor said, smiling as they exited the gas station out the front. They moved to the fuel truck. A zombie came around the trailer and Tank took care of it with the tomahawk.

"I need to get me one of these," Tank said, admiring the weapon.

"We've got a couple more back at the truck," Connor said. "Plus we saved you a couple of good guns and even a tac vest and some NVGs."

"Kick ass. You guys really are the best. It'll be like Christmas in June!"

Connor laughed as he looked at the tanker trailer. There were a bunch of nozzles, valves and stuff on the side, but what did they do?

"Figure it out?" Tank asked over his shoulder as he watched for anything that might sneak up on them.

"Hell, I don't know."

"Open 'em all up."

"Good idea."

Opening all the nozzles and turning all the valves, he finally got something to work as gas began to pour out onto the ground. He jumped back, splashing himself a little.

"Let's get back," Connor said, backing away. "How far can you throw?"

"Far enough."

They stopped at fifty yards and watched as more of the clear liquid pooled on the ground. Another thirty seconds and they could smell it from where they were standing.

"Damn, that stinks," Tank said.

"I think it's time," Connor said, handing Tank the bottle and rag.

"Let's blow it." Tank grabbed the bottle and poured some alcohol onto the cloth, then stuck it into the end of the open bottle. He looked around. "You don't happen to have a lighter, do you?"

"I didn't even think of that."

"Oh, hey, turn around." Tank unzipped his backpack on Connor's back and pulled out a nice Zippo lighter. "I wasn't going anywhere without this baby."

Lighting the cloth, Tank handed Connor the tomahawk and chucked the bottle toward the fuel truck. As soon as it left his hand, they turned and ran. The bottle crashed against the trailer and fire roared to life, igniting the gas. The whole trailer exploded and then the pumps burst into flames. It was everything Connor had ever imagined as he stood and watched the flames continue to grow, reaching into the darkening sky. The wind whipped the flames and pushed the billowing smoke to the east.

"That's awesome!" Connor said. "We need to do this again."

"Oh, hell yeah!"

Connor handed the tomahawk back to Tank and they returned to the group, still crouched behind the white building.

"I think that'll work," James said, smiling.

"Wow," Chloe said, "that was actually pretty cool."

"Never seen that before," Selena said.

"Let's go back the way we came, then get to that dealership," James said.

"'Some shine like galaxies, and some... some burn like a moth at the flame!'" Connor quoted with a smile.

"Nice," Tank said, nodding.

"*Bioshock*? Really?" Mike asked. "You guys really are nerds."

"Of course," Tank said. "What would you do stuck in a half-horse town in the middle of nowhere with nothing to do?"

"Play video games," Mike said, shrugging.

"Precisely," Tank said.

Connor followed as his brother led the group to the back side of the department store. He smiled at Tank and Mike, who bantered back and forth as they walked. Tank had a way of making light of serious situations and turning boring times interesting. With him around, sometimes it was easy to forget that this was the end of the world. Besides, why would Connor want to think about the end of the world—all the death he'd seen and brought to others, their parents gone, the hope of a new life somewhere far off in the distance, and the distinct possibility of a bloody end for all of them right around the corner. Who would want to live if that's all there was to look forward to? So Connor chose to ignore the very real fear inside and focus instead on the here and now. They were alive and they were together—the last vestiges of his friends and family from another life.

# 13
# A PERFECT STORM

James looked across the street at the used car dealership and was relieved to see that most of the zombies had moved north. They'd only have to take care of a handful moving from the south toward the flaming gas station. The wind had increased over the last half hour and was now blowing strongly, dark clouds rolling in over the mountains to the west. A storm was brewing. The light was fading. They were running out of time.

"We need to be quick. Take those zombies out and move to the building, then find the keys, get a truck, and get out of this place," James said. "That storm looks like it is gonna hit soon, and it's gonna hit hard."

"Yeah, and that fire's gonna draw zombies from all over," Connor said.

"We need to be long gone before either happens," Tank said.

James led the way across the street. A zombie turned toward him and took two steps before it fell to the ground, a spike driven into its head. Tank took one down to their left while Connor took one down to their right with his knife.

With the Wolf Pack leading, they moved across the street, taking down the dozen zombies in their way.

"Let's find a couple rides," James said as they arrived at the dealership.

"Huge sale! Today only! Everything free!" Mike said.

A dark gray truck sitting by the road caught James's attention. He walked over and looked at the Dodge RAM 2500 with a brush guard on the front. It was a crew cab and a little older than his truck, but it would work perfectly.

"Found mine," James said.

"Really?" Connor asked, walking up. "Another Dodge?"

"Of course. It's the end of the world. Nothing else will hold up."

"You keep telling yourself that."

"Oh, hell yeah!" Tank yelled from behind the dealership building.

James ran over and found Tank standing next to a black Hummer.

"I wouldn't expect you to choose anything less," James said. "Let's go find the keys."

Moving to the front of the building, James tried the door, but it was locked.

"I got this," Tank said, picking up a cinder block from next to the building and raising it over his head.

"Hey, good find!" Mike said, bending down and picking up a key that was hidden underneath.

"Oh, yeah," Tank said, setting the cinder block down.

"You had no idea that was there, did you?" James asked.

"Nope," Tank said, smiling. "I was just gonna break the front window."

James chuckled, taking the key from Mike and unlocking the door. He opened it and Tank went into the room, tomahawk at the ready.

"It's good," he said from inside. James walked through the door. "Wait! No it's not!"

A zombie crawled out from behind the counter. Tank pounced on it with the tomahawk.

"Now, it's clear," Tank said, wiping the blood from the blade.

James moved to the wall behind the counter where a bunch of keys with labels hung from hooks. Finding the two sets they needed, he tossed the keys for the Hummer to Tank and they walked outside.

"Make sure it starts and has gas," James said. "We need to split up. Who's going with who?"

"I got Tank," Connor said. "Shotgun."

"Shotgun!" Mike said.

"Then you're with me, Mike," James said. "Ladies?"

"I'll go with you," Selena said.

"Oh, I'm definitely not going with *him*," Chloe said, pointing at Tank.

"But baby, I thought we had somethin' special," Tank said, looking hurt.

"Screw off," Chloe said, walking over to the gray Dodge.

"Okay, let's go," James said, unlocking the truck and climbing in.

The truck roared to life, the gas gauge indicating it was full. Mike climbed into the passenger seat, wincing as he sat down. Chloe got into the seat behind Mike, and Selena climbed in behind James. He backed out and pulled over to the exit. Soon, Tank joined him in the black lifted Hummer that also had a brush guard.

"Oh, yeah," Tank said, rolling his window down.

"Gas?" James asked.

"Good," Connor said. "Rollin' out."

James pulled out first and Tank followed. They drove past the burning gas station and noticed the zombies walking right into the flames. Some caught sight of them and stumbled towards them like living torches. Pulling back onto the interstate, they continued north, headlights illuminating the road ahead in the growing darkness. He kept a sharp eye out for any more spike strips. The last of the light faded as raindrops began to fall, splattering on the windshield.

"This doesn't look good," Mike said.

"No, it'll be a big storm," James said.

He pulled the radio out of his vest. "Emmett, you there?"

Static. He tried again. Still nothing. James cursed, putting the radio back into a pocket on his vest.

*I don't think he would've left us, would he?*

The conversation they'd had earlier that morning made James unsure. Emmett had Alexis and Ana to take care of, and he'd put them before Connor and James. He couldn't blame him for that. James would do the same thing if it were his family. He thought about Olive and hoped she was unharmed. The safest place for her right now was with Emmett, but if something had happened to her…

"You met Tank in school, right?" Chloe asked, interrupting his thoughts.

"Yeah, in middle school."

"Where at?"

"A small town in the San Juan Mountains of Colorado."

"Has he always been... like that?"

"He's honestly a great guy. Yeah, he jokes around and acts like he hates people, but usually the meaner he is to you the more he likes you. The thing is, no matter what, he's there for his family. He has their backs and is a true friend, however unpleasant he can be at times. And true friends are hard to come by, especially these days."

"Huh, I figured he was just an ass."

"Oh no, there's a lot more to him than you realize. So how'd it go down during the ambush?" James asked, wanting to piece together what had taken place.

"All I know is one second we were getting shot at and then we crashed into that truck. I was dazed. Tank got me out and we ran. Selena was in the other truck and she ran with us. Do you know what happened to everyone else?"

"I don't, but from the looks of things I'd say they didn't make it."

Chloe looked like she was about to cry as she gazed out the window. The rain was coming down even harder now. It was becoming difficult for James to see the road and obstacles ahead. He slowed down and saw Tank do the same behind him. How far north should they go? When would they know if Emmett made it out or not? Should they turn around and go back and check to make sure they weren't in trouble? Or should they forget about the others and continue to Alaska?

"What's your story, Mike?" James asked.

"Me? I grew up in Rock Springs, Wyoming," Mike answered.

"You lose your family?"

"Yeah, something like that. Look, I don't wanna be rude. You guys did me a solid, but I don't want to talk about my past, okay?"

"That works."

"Thanks."

Lightning flashed in the dark sky ahead. James slammed on the brakes. The truck slid forward on the wet pavement. He cursed, looking back and throwing the truck into reverse. Tank had either seen the taillights or the barricade ahead because he was backing up too.

The first bullet hit the truck, shattering the passenger window and slamming into Mike's neck. Blood sprayed onto the front dash as he grasped at his neck, trying to breathe. The girls screamed. Behind, Tank swung his Hummer around and gunned it. Bullets continued to hit the truck, shattering glass and tearing through metal. James drove into a clear area and whipped the truck around, throwing it into drive and speeding off to the south. Bullets continued to fly at them from behind. The back window shattered and something thumped against his seat.

James didn't look back and he didn't slow down. He followed the taillights in front of him and prayed they wouldn't hit another spike strip on the road somewhere. His side hurt, feeling warm and wet, but he didn't take his hands off the wheel to check it.

Rain flew through the shattered windshield and in the side windows, pelting his face. He could feel at least a dozen small cuts, and blood trickled down into his mouth. Next to him, Mike was still alive but was having a hard time stemming the flow of blood.

"Give him your coat!" James yelled at the girls in the back.

Surprisingly, Chloe was the one to act, taking off her jacket and reaching up to put it against Mike's neck. He let go of the wound for a second to put the jacket in place and blood squirted from his neck.

*He's not going to make it.*

Ahead, James was beginning to lose Tank's taillights. Barely able see as the rain speckled his glasses and blood ran down his face, he gunned it. How had the bastards known they were coming? And who the hell were these people? The Reclaimers? That meant nothing to him. He'd only ever heard of them from Mike.

The questions nagged at him, but he could do nothing about them, so he drove on. Endless darkness loomed ahead. He'd lost Tank's taillights and the truck was beginning to slow even though he pushed the pedal to the floor. Was the gas running out, or was it something worse? He glanced over and saw Chloe was in the back seat again and Mike slumped in the passenger seat, his hands no longer covering his wound.

"Help him!" James roared.

"He's dead," Chloe said, a quiver in her voice. "They both are."

James cursed and the engine started to make odd noises as smoke poured from under the hood.

"I can't see them!" Connor said, looking back. "Slow down!"

"Got it," Tank said.

"Son of bitch! Were they just waiting for us?"

"I told you, bro, they *hounded* us that night we got away. I was sure when we doubled back they'd find us in that house."

Connor watched through the back window, but he still couldn't see his brother's headlights.

*Dammit! Is the whole universe against us?*

Connor looked around. They'd only been hit by a few rounds—one of the back windows had a hole in it and there were a few holes in the hood, but nothing serious.

"Stop, we need to wait for them," Connor said.

Tank pulled next to an abandoned box truck and turned the Hummer off, along with all the dome and dash lights. They were plunged into complete darkness. Rain pounded on the roof and lightning illuminated the sky at random intervals.

They waited for a couple of minutes. Still no James.

"We need to go back," Connor said.

JOSHUA C. CHADD

"You ready to kick some ass if we have to?" Tank asked as he started the Hummer and turned around.

"I'm always ready to kick some ass."

Headlights shone on abandoned vehicles as they made their way back. Connor kept his eyes open, searching for enemies and zombies but especially for his brother and the gray truck. Why did this keep happening to them? Were they being punished? Or was this just what the new world was like—one disaster right after another. It was like Murphy's Law had come to life. Connor tightened his grip on the AR in his hands.

*You better not be dead, bro!*

Minutes passed and there was still no sign of James or the truck. Connor was beginning to lose hope that they'd ever find him. If he'd crashed off the side of the road, they would never see him in the darkness with this storm. Then what would he do? He had Tank sure, but Tank—however much his brother—was not James. Could he live without the one person who'd been there his whole life? Could he continue on without him?

"There!" Tank said, pointing to the gray Dodge sitting in the middle of the interstate, smoke rising from under the hood. All the windows were shattered and bullet holes speckled the entire vehicle. "That doesn't look good."

*Don't you even think of leaving me!* Connor thought, fighting his emotions.

Tank pulled the Hummer in a circle, coming to a stop facing south on the right side of the Dodge. Connor opened the door, rain blowing inside. Jumping out and quickly shutting the door, he ran over to the truck, soaked by the time he arrived. Mike slumped in the passenger seat, a gaping wound in his neck. He looked into the backseat and noticed Selena bent forward, leaning on her seatbelt with a small hole in the back of her head and most of her face missing. Jumping back, he reacted as Mike's corpse began to stir. Without thinking, he pulled out his knife and stabbed it in the eye. He shoved the knife back into its sheath without wiping off the blade as he looked around.

*Where the hell are you, James?*

Movement behind an abandoned vehicle at the edge of the light cast by the Hummer's headlights made him turn. It was a large zombie limping toward them.

"Damn you, James! Where are you?"

He was angry and just wanted to kill something. Spinning, he sighted in on the zombie with his ACOG, his finger resting on the trigger, but he quickly lowered his AR and ran forward. It was no zombie. James was supporting Chloe as they staggered toward the Hummer. Connor took Chloe from his brother, who was holding his side, and began to walk her back to the Hummer.

"Thanks," Chloe said, wincing as he took her.

"You good, bro?" Connor asked, worry plain in his voice.

"Yeah, hit in the side. Not sure how bad," James said, breathing heavily.

Connor helped Chloe into the backseat and then went around to the other side and opened the door for his brother. James climbed in. Connor jumped into the passenger's seat and Tank sped off, heading south again.

"Good to see you two," Tank said. "The others?"

"Didn't make it," James said, looking down at his side.

He unzipped his tactical vest, taking it off and pulling his shirt up. A small piece of metal was stuck in his left side. He touched it. It wasn't in deep so he pulled it out, wincing at the pain.

"You got the first aid—"

Connor already had the kit open. "Chloe, you good?"

"Yeah, I just twisted my ankle when I jumped out of the truck."

Connor handed James a clean piece of gauze and he wiped off most of the blood. As wounds went, it wasn't bad—basically just a large cut. No organs had been damaged. He'd probably be fine, but it hurt like hell.

Connor helped him wrap his side after they'd cleaned and sterilized it, and it felt much better now that he'd removed the metal shard. He leaned his head back and closed his eyes.

"Where the hell do we go?" Tank asked. "We're boxed in."

"Turn off on one of the roads opposite Sheridan," James said. "Get off the grid and figure out what these bastards want."

"Too late," Tank said. "Just passed the exit for US-14."

"Let's whip it around then," James said. His ear and side were beginning to hurt more now that the adrenaline was fading.

The hummer began to turn. "Stop!" Connor said.

Tank pressed on the brakes and the Hummer slid to a stop.

"What?" Tank asked.

"James," Connor said.

By the tone of his voice, James knew it was bad—very bad. He opened his eyes and looked out the windshield. Sitting in the middle of the interstate was the other school bus.

*Please no,* James thought. *I can't bear it if they're all dead.*

He climbed out of the Hummer, flicking on the flashlight attached to his AR. The rain had abated somewhat, but was still coming down in sheets. Connor joined him and they slowly approached the bus, wary of any traps.

James looked at the bus. Suddenly it was on fire, children screaming from inside the inferno. He could see Olive in there as the skin melted off her face. Mila sat next to her, clutching her little body in charred arms. She looked up at him with those hazel eyes, an expression of pure horror and pain on her face.

Just as suddenly, he was in the master bedroom, and blood covered every surface. The half-eaten bodies of fifteen children were scattered on the floor. The zombie that had been Sandy crouched over one of the bodies, ripping off chunks of flesh. It looked up at James, fresh blood smeared on its face, and lunged for him.

When he came back to himself, he was on all fours on the pavement, rain pouring down around him. Connor was kneeling next to him with a hand on his back. James looked up at his brother, the rain hiding his tears. Connor's face was a mask of concern.

"What just happened?" Connor asked, uncharacteristically gentle.

"I have no idea," James said, picking up his AR and standing. "It was like that time in the basement, but worse. I don't know what's going on."

"How do you feel now?"

"Terrified, but alive. Let's check the bus."

"I don't know if that's a good idea."

"Connor, I'm fine. Let's go."

James passed his brother and walked to the bus. The door was open and he climbed in, looking around. There were no zombies and, surprisingly, only one body slumped against the back door. Slowly walking down the center aisle, a feeling of unease grew inside him. He heard Connor enter the bus behind him, but he didn't look back.

The body was one of the men. Hank, he thought. He was completely naked, a metal stake driven through his head and into the back door. "I have been reclaimed" was written in blood on the back window above his head. Inside his mouth a folded piece of paper, which James pulled out and unfolded. The feeling of unease had grown into pure dread.

A crude map was drawn on the paper with a red X marking a spot somewhere east of the interstate. He flipped it over. Words in red ink were written in a flowing script.

James read the note aloud, "I have your friends. I will kill one every twelve hours until you arrive. Come unarmed and in plain sight. If I even *think* you're planning a rescue, I'll kill them all, starting with the little ones. You have to pay for what you've done, the lives you've taken. I'm waiting, J."

# EPILOGUE

A door swung open and light flooded the dirt floor. Alexis's eyes snapped wide. She blinked, trying to adjust to the sudden brightness of the lights from outside the doorway. Looking around, she saw that all the adults, including Ana, were chained to wooden posts driven into the ground. Everyone's wrists were clasped in metal shackles behind their backs, and the shackles were then chained to the posts. The large room appeared to be the inside of a pole barn with metal walls and a simple dirt floor.

*Wait, where's dad?* she thought, panicking as she searched the shadows, but he wasn't there. *Where is he? Did they kill him?* She racked her brain, trying to remember what had happened and how they'd come to be there. Her thoughts were blurry and the back of her head hurt. She'd been hit in the head. She knew that much, but what had happened?

Her eyes were drawn to two figures standing outside, illuminated by an exterior light above the door. Their backs were turned, but they were armed and looked to be male. Beyond them, the sky was beginning to darken. This startled her.

*How long have we been here? And who are these people?*

A different figure strode into the room, backlit by the light flooding in from outside. Alexis couldn't make out much about this person because of the shadows. The figure stepped further into the room and approached her, crouching down in front of her and looking her in the eyes. Alexis was shocked by the face that stared at her—a beautiful woman with pretty blue eyes and a face framed by luscious black hair.

"Hello, my dear," the woman said, caressing Alexis's cheek. "Did you sleep well?"

"Where are we?" Alexis asked. The woman had a sweet voice. Everything about her made Alexis feel at ease.

*This is so wrong. Who is she?*

"Your new home," she said and paused, looking thoughtful. "More like a temporary home, actually. I wouldn't get too attached."

"Who are you?" Alexis asked.

"Who am I? That's rude," the woman said. "You haven't even told me your name."

"Alexis."

"Now that's better. You can call me Jezz."

Her voice was so sweet and her smile so genuine that Alexis was completely caught off guard. *This must be the person they send to talk to the prisoners,* she thought, *to put them at ease.*

"Where are all the kids?" Alexis asked, the realization of their absence hitting her as she looked around the room.

"They're safe. I couldn't really keep them in a place like this, now could I?"

"Why are we here?" Alexis asked, looking back at Jezz.

"Ah, now that's a good question—one I can't answer quite yet. We're waiting on more guests to arrive."

"Guests?"

"Yes, my dear."

"Guests for what?"

"You'll see, but don't fret about that now."

"Do you know where my father is?" Alexis found herself asking before she could stop. The question had been nagging on her mind since she'd awakened.

"Your father?" Jezz asked.

"One of the men with us. He's not here."

"Ah, which one? The one I staked to the back of the bus? Or do you mean the two young men we're waiting on?" Jezz asked, a wicked smile twisting her face. Gone was the sweet woman, replaced by a creature who had a maniacal look in her eyes and an evil grin.

Alexis was taken aback.

"Yes, I know about your friends, but don't worry. They'll be heading this way shortly. We can't have them leaving and ruining all the fun."

"What do you mean 'fun'? We're prisoners here!" Ana said, from across the barn.

"Ah, there's the fiery redhead from earlier," Jezz said and walked over to Ana.

"Why the façade?" Ana asked. "You've already caught us. Why keep this up?"

"Façade?" Jezz asked, standing in front of Ana. "You misunderstand all of this. I'm doing this for you."

"How can you even say that?"

"Because I mean it. But I don't expect someone simple-minded like you to be able to understand it."

Jezz walked back over to Alexis and reached down to caress her cheek, but Alexis instinctively shied away.

"Oh, don't worry my dear. I'm not going to hurt you—at least not yet." She walked to the door and looked back. "This is for your own good, trust me. You'll see soon enough."

"You're demented!" Ana screamed as Jezz turned her back and walked through the door.

One of the guards shut the door behind her, plunging the room into darkness.

"Now what'd we do?" Ana asked, struggling with the shackles.

"Wait, I guess. James and Connor will be coming for us soon and we still don't know where my dad is," Alexis said.

"Yeah, but this woman's insane. What's to say she won't randomly just kill us all?"

"Nothing."

Ana sighed, renewing her efforts to escape her bonds.

Alexis could hear some of the men and women around her crying and cursing. She tried to stand, but her wrists were fastened tight and the chain was too short to offer much movement. There was no way she was going to be able to fight back or break free. They were stuck here until they were rescued or killed, yet she felt an odd sense of peace. She couldn't explain it and it didn't make any sense, but she felt calm, like everything was going to work out and they had nothing to worry about. Maybe it was her exhausted mind playing tricks on her or sleep deprivation, but she felt they weren't alone. It was almost as if there was someone watching over them, protecting them.

She leaned her head back against the pole she was chained to. Maybe she was finally losing it. After all she'd been through in the past week, she could see how that could happen. It'd be so easy for her to break and never even know it. All of this could be a horrible nightmare for all she knew. But no, this was real. Too real. She decided to believe the presence was really there—and it was there to help them. She chose to believe, despite the fears and doubts gnawing at her, despite the knowledge that she may die soon, unable to do anything about it. She believed.

*This is not the end,* said an unfathomable voice in her mind.

# ACKNOWLEDGEMENTS

As always, I couldn't have finished this book without the help of numerous people. Huge thanks to:

Jesus, you've guided me every step along this journey, in writing and in life.

My wife, you're the catalyst that pushed me to pursue this lifestyle. You've spent countless hours with me proofing, editing, helping with the cover, website, and everything else. I couldn't have done this without you!

My family, you've continued to support and help me through the whole process.

Guildies in the FRG, you helped out more than I can say! You've transformed this story from something barely palatable to the epic it is!

My awesome editor, without you this would read like a third grader wrote it. Your skills and time are highly appreciated!

My cover artist, you had to put up with a lot, but you worked hard and made the skin for my book look badass!

And finally to all my readers, you're the ones who keep me going and allow me to chase this dream! Thank you for all the past and future success!

## ABOUT THE AUTHOR

I am a Jesus Freak and follower of the Way. As an adventurous nerd, I love the outdoors and when I'm not found high in the mountains of Alaska, I can be observed living on the rolling plains of eastern Montana with my wife, guns, and two katanas. I have a passion for all things imaginary and find inspiration in the wilderness, away from all the distractions of life. Some of my other passions include hunting, shooting, board and video games, hard rock, movies, reading, and the Walking Dead.

Learn more about me at:
*www.joshuacchadd.com*

Also by Joshua C. Chadd

**The Brother's Creed Series**
*Outbreak*
*Battleborn*
*Wolf Pack (2018)*

51084179R00141

Made in the USA
San Bernardino, CA
12 July 2017